SUNSET SUNRISE MY TURN ON EARTH

Gilbert R. Williamson

COUNTRY BOOKS

Published by: Country Books
Courtyard Cottage, Little Longstone, Bakewell, Derbyshire DE45 1NN
for:
Gilbert R. Williamson
7 Kaimes Place, Kirknewton, Midlothian EH27 8AX

ISBN 1 898941 14 9
© 1998 G.R. Williamson
Text and photos

British Library Cataloguing in Publication Data:
a catalogue record for this book is available from the British Library.

DEDICATION:
To my parents

ACKNOWLEDGEMENTS:
I would like to thank friends for helping me to compile this book. For those who guided me
through the labyrinth of the publishing business, for those who read the manuscript and made
useful suggestions, encouraging me to go the whole way towards publication.

Design and production by:
Dick Richardson, Country Books

Printed in England by:
MFP Design & Print, Stretford, Manchester M32 0JT

Colour origination by:
GA Graphics, Stamford, Lincolnshire PE9 2RB

CONTENTS

CHAPTER 1

My Turn on Earth

School takes up a lot of time in a child's life. My first school, primary school, was Wardie, a fine modern building on the north of the city off Granton Road. It had an inner courtyard with the classrooms, offices and gym built on the outside in the shape of a rectangle. I was not clever at school. My problem was that whenever I sat down in a comfortable room I just started dreaming. I have never got over this even when older but am more likely now to fall asleep. The only thing that stopped me from falling asleep at school was fear of chastisement from the teacher. I would have been quiet, not talking to neighbours, seeming to be attentive, but I was not. The result was I learned nothing and this showed up in my exam marks. I did like drawing and when the time came I would pick up my drawing materials with enthusiasm and the teacher one day noticing this looked me straight in the eye and said, "You like drawing don't you". I thought what a very nice teacher Miss Gray was. The head mistress was a big buxom woman who made her presence known wherever she was, speaking always in a loud voice. The head master was a small, erect man, always in a dark suit. My encounter with him was not a pleasant one. Some of us became under the influence of Satan and decided to steal marbles from the pockets of boys' jackets hanging in the cloakroom. What possessed us to do it, I do not know, but of course we were found out and brought before the headmaster. It was a right upturn and the janitor made his contribution by saying we were a "disgrace to the school". A letter was sent to our parents and I was chastised severely by my mother by being shown into the bedroom, my trousers taken down and lashed on my bare bottom, using a leather strap. It was a very effective deterrent. I can assure you I have never done it again.

I was eleven years old in May 1939 and war began in September of that year. I was in my last year in primary school and when the school was closed for a time because of the emergency, we met in a house, being taught by the headmaster, about 6 or 8 of us in the class enough to fill the room. One afternoon remains firmly in my mind. During the class, gun fire was heard and on looking out of the window little puffs of white smoke could be seen in the sky like parachutes falling and when we were let out of school, still the shells were exploding in the sky. It was a practice we were told. Later in the day a large bomber aircraft appeared just above the roof tops over the Pilton estate chased by two smaller fighter planes. There was a burst of machine gun fire from a battery off Ferry Road not far away. Quite spectacular, some did not believe it was a practice and they were right, for on the 6 o'clock news that night, it was announced that the first air raid by the Germans had taken place over the Firth of Forth that day. So we were watching the real thing, there had been no warning.

I am afraid my behaviour was not much better at secondary school, dreaming was still my occupation. Trinity Academy was over a mile from home and a group of us would walk there every morning, that was until I got my pushbike, a present from my parents. I spent many years on that bike and improvements and modifications were carried over the years. We had nick names for our teachers such as Cowboy Smith, Turpy, Squeak, (spoke with a very small voice), Weary, the head master, Cat-in-the-bag, etc. One teacher, I forget her name, used to call for silence by saying 'I want to hear myself stink'. There were frequent references to the war and one teacher would break off from the maths lesson, full of emotion, arms going in the air, 'we will win, we must win, we are right, boys and girls, we will win the war'. All inspiring stuff except for those in the first two seats who were likely to be spat on during the outburst.

I don't remember passing out with anything special when leaving school. I have always enjoyed music and one teacher began a recorder band. I bought the penny whistle but the teacher never followed it through. One song I will always remember singing was 'Who were the yeomen the yeomen of England'. We would sing it with gusto even as Scotsmen. The school was divided into 'homes' Royston, Bangholm, Warriston and Craighall, I was in the latter. We never won much but we did win the singing competition. We had the local tuck shop to sustain us between meals and the headmaster would talk to us during the interval from the steps of the gym when any announcements had to be made. The poor man lost his wife during this time and he could not talk about her without breaking down, we felt sorry for him. Gymnastics was always fun. One teacher kept a belt over his shoulder under his jacket and out it would come with the speed of light if he thought someone needed encouragement. Yes, we got the belt once, twice or thrice and sore it was too, but something worse was the ruler on the back of the legs. The shear anticipation of it coming was enough to make you squeal. The French teacher would often say to us dreamers, 'boy come back to earth' when a pupil's attention had wandered elsewhere. Flucker fell asleep on the back row of the class and was asked to occupy a seat in front of the teacher so she could keep an eye on him. She then began to say the French were a very logical people, the French word for skyscraper was something or other which literally meant it scratches the sky, very logical indeed. However, Flucker left the earth again for another planet as indicated by his snoring in front of her which left the teacher merely scratching her head.

Playtime is very important for children. It's when they can do their own thing, make their own friends, exercise their talents, be themselves. It's bound up with a desire for freedom from authority. A favourite game for us boys and girls in the street was 'kick the can'. An empty can was placed in the centre of the road, someone gave it a good kick and another pre-selected unfortunate ran after it, and brought it back to the original spot. While this was done, the rest of us ran away to hide and then he had to look for us. If we were discovered, we were in the den, but we could be released by someone undiscovered kicking the can again. When all of us were found, the game was over. A plank of wood on pram wheels was called a guider and many hours were spent making and playing on our guiders. My friend had one which ran on ball-bearings and a slight push would take him to the shops half a mile away without additional effort, a slight downhill helping things along. Before that, I used to push an old car tyre and cast-offs from my father's car were eagerly awaited to change my mode of transport so to speak. and other boys had a steel hoop which they would propel along with a ring bar attachment. One day my chum and I were playing with a wooden ball, rolling it back and forth to each other, when my friend missed his catch, and the ball went rolling along down the street. Another of our friends was seen walking up the street so we shouted on him to kick the ball. When his foot made contact with the wooden ball he let out such a yell. I squirm even now when I think about it, and how cruel children can be to one another. One of the more criminal activities we got up to was to place a stink bomb in a letter box. Bombs were made by wrapping paper round a roll of 35mm film and setting it alight. It did not go on fire, but gave off a lot of smoke and pungent smell. Three of us were involved, one supplied the film, one of us set it alight, and one of us placed it in the letter box opening. People gathered around when they saw smoke coming from the box expecting perhaps a genie to appear but all that appeared was three fire engines ready to deal with the situation. Some letters were scorched, but none went on fire. The police took no action. Marbles were very popular when I was a boy those small glass balls in all sorts of attractive colours readily available from the local shop. Different games were played using them. Conkers (horse chestnuts) in season were sought after and dangling on the end of a piece of string were used to contest others. Bully tens and more were not uncommon. Pevery Beds, the squares chalked out on the pavement and the empty ointment tin slid into each square in turn as we hopped, skipped and jumped missing one each time. The peery tops spun around with a rod and leather strap with chalk marks on the top making an attractive design as the faster it went. Another time us boys were on our cycles in the street when we saw a man sitting on the ground between the posts of his garden gate. He seemed unable to get up and had managed to somehow jam himself between the posts. He was sitting right angles to the pavement with his back against one post and his foot and toe against the other. We did not feel that physically we could go to his aid but something had to be done. Just as we were contemplating this a lady, living two doors up, came walking along the street and she was a very fine lady indeed. Wearing a tight fitting coat with a high fur collar she carried herself well and was always dressed to perfection. We wondered what her reaction would be when she saw the unfortunate fellow in his predicament. But she merely looked down then looked up and walked on without even the hint of a hesitation in her step almost as if she had been trained how to deal with such a situation. So with no help from her what should we do? We decided to throw small stones at the window to attract the attention of the inhabitants of the household so they might observe this member of the family blocking the entrance to the establishment. This brought two or three people to the window who subsequently came out and helped the man into the house.

It must not be thought we had many drunks in the street, it was a middle class neighbourhood where people were reasonably well off and drunkenness was not a problem.

'School days are the happiest days of your life', so they say, but I don't agree. Some teachers seemed to be appalled when they realised one of us boys was nearing the end of his school days. To go out into life, having learning nothing, in their opinion, filled them with misgiving. But the education at school is only part of the education for life. I feel that schools, colleges and universities are places where knowledge of a particular subject is pumped into pupils and that is all. I think it was the Duke of Wellington who said that "education has for its object the formation of character". I really believed this for a time and assumed he was referring to the institutions mentioned above but my experiences of them is not so. I spent too long I believe in further education, but it was the thing in those days. Get yourself a good job, a job for life, a secure job, with a good pension, that was the thing. Today things are different. I read recently that one now can expect to change their job three times in the course of a working life. I was never very excited about security and insurance policies very much tied up with security. The words of Peter Ustinoff always rang true with me, "security, who want security, security is death". But I will have to accept that for some security would give them a happy life. I do believe that the object of education is the formation of character but that is the education in the great university of life.

My education began when I joined the Boy Scouts or rather the cubs at the age of 8 years. There were always tests to pass, things to do, activities and games. We had four leaders in the cubs all ladies Akela, Baloo, Bagheera, and Carr. "A-ka-la we'll do our best, we'll dib, dib, dib, dib, we'll dob, dob, dob, woof". So we would end the night formed in a circle round the Akela or leader. It was an orderly one hour and it taught us young boys discipline. Our Akela or leader lived in a large house and in her equally expansive garden was a large apple tree. One summer evening she took the Pack to her home and let us loose on the tree which was heavily laden with lovely red apples. During my exertions to get my share the braces on my pants parted company and I looked a strange sight as I made my way home hanging on to my apples and pants at the same time. Then moving on to the Scouts at the age eleven. The meeting began by breaking the flag followed by inspection then games, activities, tests ending with a game or campfire, lowering the flag, closing prayer then 'good night Scouts'. Then there were hikes, week-end camps, summer camp, church parades, visit by the District Commissioner, football tournaments and the District Shield Competition a test on all scouting skills. Also the occasional Gang Show and parents night. I was invested as a Rover Scout the day before I was called up for National Service. I well remember the arm falling on my left shoulder as part of the initiation ceremony. Two years later we met to form the Crew. Much to my surprise I was made Rover Mate. I had no idea what to do and simply ran off and no one came after me. It may have been partly that but also I was going through a re-think on religion and the role of the church in time of war. I stayed away from the church for a number of years. We had just gone through a period of bitter conflict lasting nearly five years between countries who considered themselves Christian. How did this square with the concept of love for all mankind. Now if you are attacked that is different you must defend yourself, but the policy of war and the pursuit of war towards some end or purpose is a dangerous one for Christian peoples to follow.

CHAPTER 2

Education for Life

I once met a man who had been a Scoutmaster but had left the Scouts because he could not obey the Scout Promise. I was puzzled. It says, 'I promise on my honour that I will do my best to do my duty to God and the Queen . . .' It was this last bit that he could not reconcile because he said the desires of God and that of the Queen and country may be different. I had never thought about it in this way and I could sympathise with his views. However, the Church is not perfect, but it does a lot of good and provides worthwhile activities for individuals to pursue. Without the church the world would be a poorer place and without youth activities, boys would simply form themselves into gangs and pursue mischief. Looking back now I regret my inactivity during those youthful years. I can't confess to having done anything drastic during this time but my life was pretty negative. I was working as an apprentice motor mechanic and was attending Night School studying Mechanical Engineering. I also went to a Day School once a week to learn the workings of the Internal Combustion Engine. I returned to church activities again and Scouting in 1955. One incident remains in my mind during my period of inactivity. My mother had bought me a very loud tie, one of many colours, I put it on one day and when I was walking down the road I met the minister. Now I had not seen him for a very long time, perhaps even years, when we approached, I said 'hello'. He did not look at me, but at the tie, returned the, 'hello', and walked on. Scouting became a hobby for me over the next six years and I loved it. When you join a scout troop you have immediately won for yourself 30 friends and good friends at that. I can't profess to having made a very auspicious start to my new career. When I entered the church hall a number of scouts were playing a game which came to an end shortly after my arrival. One of the senior boys came up to me and said, 'what game shall we play now sir'. I had not a clue, the only game I could remember from my early days was British Bulldog. I suggested playing this when he replied, 'we've just finished playing that sir'. I obtained a warrant as an Assistant Scout Master and ran the troop with another assistant who was the minister's son who had asked me to help him run the troop and so I could say my education had re-started.

The big event of the year for the scouts is the summer camp. You could say all activities during the winter months are in preparation for this camp. It was advisable to pick the camp site the year before so that during the winter months we could 'advertise' the camp, pin point its geographical location, produce a map of the site and so on. There was also weekend camps to break the boys in. The Scouts motto is "Be Prepared", and it is more than good advice when going to camp. A year's preparation is not too long and it will ensure a successful camp even if the weather lets you down. Our mode of transport was a large van to convey boys and equipment to the site. One of the biggest items of equipment was the straw box. One of the most difficult things to cook was porridge. Now I love porridge, but porridge with lumps makes me boak and one way to avoid this was the straw box. The porridge was brought to the boil the night before, the pan placed in the box to allow the contents to cook overnight, in the morning it only needed warming to produce lovely creamy porridge.

Our camp sites were in the Borders and the Highlands of Scotland. The morning would be spent travelling and after arriving at the site and unloading the equipment eat our sandwiches before setting up camp. This would take the whole of the afternoon then after tea would spend time with the troop walking around the immediate vicinity of the camp site to, as it were, get our bearings. Scouts were never really settled in until after a night's sleep although sleep on the first night was sometimes difficult. I remember on one occasion a fight started between two rival tents when aluminium eating utensils were flung through the air at each other, quite serious if a spinning plate caught you on the head. One patrol would be on cooking duties for 24 hours coming on at supper time to tea time the next day. Other patrols would gather wood for the fire, dig the latrines, clean up the camp site and maybe obtain supplies from the nearest shop. After dinner a wide game, some scouts were good at thinking up ideas for this. After tea the scouts were on free time until supper which might include a camp fire and songs. Following breakfast we usually held a 'Court of Honour' a high sounding title for a meeting between the scouters and patrol leaders to map out the programme for the day ahead. We had a programme of course already prepared, but the weather might cause us to make alterations to this. Following this meeting each scout had to have his belongings and equipment laid out for inspection by the scouters visiting each tent. These preliminaries over the scouts could then turn their attention to the morning duties.

We worked closely with the guides attached to our church and when we moved out of the camp they moved in. This co-operation benefited us, as well as them, improving our cooking utensils to a much higher standard. We enjoyed these camps enormously, making preparation a lot of work, look forward to the camp itself, a week or so in the open air amid beautiful scenery and after it is over a good feeling of a job well done.

There were many amusing incidents. One I recall when we were camping in the Border region in a long field which ran east and west. A herd of cows remained in the east end of the field all day while we camped in the middle. As the sun set in the west the herd of cows moved slowly through the camp site to the west end of the park causing damage to tents tramping on articles and utensils and nearly every night the latrine screens were brought down. We were reluctant to post scouts on duty as they had free time in the evening. In the morning of course the same thing happened as the sun worshippers greeted the rising sun in the east. It meant one of us scouters getting up early to chase the herd through the camp site. Well this morning I am on duty, I roll my pyjama trouser legs to prevent them getting wet in the morning dew, arm myself with a stick, wave it above my head and generally make a scene to frighten the animals. through the camp site. Now in the kitchen area we had two pits dug into the ground where we threw rubbish, a wet pit and a dry pit. The wet pit was called a grease pit and it was covered with fern leaves which made it an excellent booby trap for the unwary. Unfortunately this animal fell into the grease pit, with one front leg in the hole causing it to lean over like a half sunken ship. It was unable to extract itself and as I moved in closer to offer what help I could it plainly wanted no help, snorting and waving its head about in an exaggerated manner. While I stood watching pondering my next move the animal gave a mighty heave and managed to extract its leg from the hole and place it on level ground again, took off at high speed towards the herd, no doubt quite determined never to enter a scouts kitchen area ever again.

Another incident happened when we were camping in the north in the Central Highlands area of the country. I usually went to the tents last thing at night to see that all the boys were there and to wish them good night. This was the last night of a week's stay and my two assistants said could they go round the tents and wish the scouts good night instead of me. I was a little surprised but said that would be all right. They went off and never came back. I waited for what I thought was sufficient time and then made a move towards the first tent. All was quiet there but not all the boys were present. I then went to the second tent and there was a proper party going on there. I waited for a while before making a move and then I shouted at the top of my voice "EVERYBODY OUT AND BACK TO YOUR TENTS". Well, there was a scatter of scouts in every direction, from under the tent valances and into the dark night. I then went into the tent to see that everybody was there, that should have been there. Having put that right I went back to the first tent and walking in the long grass I was startled by a boy who jumped up in front of me. I was walking straight in his path and if he had not made himself known I would have fallen over him. "Get back to your tent Martin, I will speak to you in the morning", I said. Arriving back at the scouters tent only one assistant was there. 'Where is John?', I asked him. 'Don't know', came the reply. I then went to the door of the tent and thought I heard someone walking and whistling towards us. The whistling grew louder and then I shouted, 'is

14

that you John?', it was him. 'Were you over in that tent?'. 'What'! 'Get inside, I will speak to you in the morning'.

I never did refer to the matter again. I was not going to have the camp end on a sour note. I only felt afterwards if the older boys had wanted a late night and had asked they could have used the hospital tent but I did not want the older boys mixing with the younger ones.

While camping in Glen Lyon, eight miles up the longest Glen in Scotland, one of the boys, a patrol leader fell and cut his leg rather badly which meant rushing him to hospital in Aberfeldy. After stitches and bandage we took him back to camp and he spent the rest of the time walking about with a straight leg. After camp was over, I thought I should go and see his parents to explain what had happened and to see how he was. I had never met them before, they were not members of the church, but they welcomed me in and I was given the best chair in the room. The boy's mum and dad were present and his older sister who seemed to do all the work in the house, but the boy himself was not there. Also a couple from Canada were in the room. The parents were very matter-of-fact about the incident and were saying it's a wonder he came home with a leg at all. He was a very energetic little fellow, and nothing got him down. During my time with them it became apparent that the adults were members of a religious sect whose membership depended on a St.Paul's type of conversion. Several times the men would throw their arms about each other and recall the day when the blinding light hit them. Whether this was done for my benefit or not I did not know. I felt they did not want me to leave. Well, time came for tea and buns and when I received mine I took a sip of tea when someone said, 'shall we say grace?'. I nearly spat it out again. When grace had been said, the young lady, seeing my embarrassment said, 'What did you say at camp, grub up boys?' Of course we always did say grace before meals at camp. I felt quite at home in their company in spite of, to me, rather strange behaviour of the men.

One of the highlights of my years with the scouts was our winning of the District Shield Competition. Each troop sends in one patrol who are subject to testing of their scouting skills. One year we were third and the patrol leader was quite determined that next year we would be first. Shortly before the competition, we held a jumble sale which raised I remember £35.00p. This enabled us to buy two hike tents, ropes, equipment and utensils so the boys went to camp with virtually everything new. I was not allowed to take part and in fact it was another District which organised the event to ensure complete fairness. I went out on the Sunday afternoon but I could detect little from the faces of the scouters as to how the competition had gone. When the announcement was made that we had won, we were over the moon. It was the same weekend as our church building was opened after being closed for several months for renovation, so it was a double celebration.

One regret was that I never obtained the Wood Badge. I did what was called the Preliminary Training Course for the Wood Badge which included four nights at a hall in the city and a weekend camp. I loved those Friday nights, you never knew what activities they had planned for you including talks, skills, teaching games, keeping you on your toes, a very lively two hours. I remember the camp being held in very frosty weather but we had plenty to do to keep us warm. I remember too a photograph being taken at the end of the course and a leader saying you could put a board over our heads we were all the same height. I have never seen that photograph.

Often I would go camping on my own and spend a weekend once in Glen Lyon where it gets very dark at night. I read a lot about the Highlands and the friendly people there and it was just as well because the inky darkness in the Glen can be a bit scary. On one occasion arriving at Lochearnhead it began to rain very heavy followed by a thunderstorm, the bands of lightening were reaching the water surface of the Loch. There was no way I was going to camp out that night so I looked for a bed and breakfast. Calling at a cottage, mid-way down the Loch, an old man answered saying the owners were out but he thought it would be all right if I could call back. Going on further, I reached the far end of the Loch and waited there. I could see guests through the window of an hotel being served a meal and then the lights going out and candles being lit. I waited for what I thought was sufficient time and returned to the cottage, the rain was so heavy, I waited in the car hoping it would ease off. However, there was a flash of fork lightening which seemed to surround the car accompanied by a clap of thunder enough to waken the dead. I lost no time in getting out, walking to the gate, up the path to the front door and to hear a friendly voice ring out, 'come in'. I then stepped into a warm and comfortable room being welcomed by the young couple. I did not sleep well that night because the old man next door kept coughing so I got up to look out of the attic window. I thought I might see some reflection off the Loch or may be an outline of some of the white hulled yachts moored off shore, but no, although the storm was over only an inky darkness presented itself. That 'scene' has remained with me ever since the absence of light had removed all traces of what would have been a pretty picture in day time.

After three years with the troop we obtained a Scoutmaster. This man came into the district and joined the church and had held this position before elsewhere. My colleague of three years decided to leave to concentrate on his theology studies. So we had a new partnership but unfortunately it did not last long. I had come to know the boys quite well over the years and they looked to me more than the new man and so he never really settled in. He wanted me to be the new leader and made this recommendation and so I became Scoutmaster with one assistant, one service auxiliary and a troop leader. I had secretly wanted this position feeling that my three years apprenticeship entitled me to the job. The minister held a meeting with the older boys when my name was put forward and accepted. The process then began in filling in a form to apply for a warrant. I was excited at first but I soon realised what a responsibility I had taken on. The success or otherwise of the troop now lay squarely on my shoulders. If it succeeded, fine, if not, disaster, and for all to see, it was a sobering thought. It has sometimes been said if a Scoutmaster knew what he was doing in taking 20 or 30 boys to camp he would never do it. However, I buried myself in the work, read as much as I could, and just worked at it. I think what compensates is the fellowship with the boys and it is a healthy relationship. One cannot be good at everything and you need ideas to keep the boys interested. One of the surprising things I read about running a scout troop is 'to let the boys run it themselves'. Now this seemed a bit foolhardy to me but when I thought about it, there is no more livelier minds than youths, we are talking about ages 15 to 18, and if you use their ideas and apply them in a constructive way it will become their troop, they will feel involved and the support will grow. We did have a difficult time when the parents committee decided to have a sale of work to raise funds for both scouts and guides. The scouts were given the task

17

of making baskets and it meant basket work on Friday nights, right up until the time of the sale. I saw the numbers go down and down. Fortunately the sale was a success and we reached our target financially, and then began the task of building the troop up again. After one year, my one assistant decided to take up night school on a Friday night so I was on my own. I felt I could do my task but assistants are necessary so that they can make their contribution. No one man can do it all himself. There was one other warranted assistant but he would not come to the meetings and gave no reason why. So I struggled on, then one night I was agreeably surprised when three young scouters from a neighbouring troop came down to the hall and took over the meeting. Two of these assistants stayed with me and so we had turned a difficult corner. Someone must have heard our cry for help and my prayers were answered.

It must not be assumed that everything in the scouts runs smoothly. There were questions about leadership, not at the very top but within our group. It did not bother me and I had good support from the District Commissioner and I was happy getting on with my job of running the troop. The D.C. was a very imposing figure, tall, slim, wore the uniform well, and made frequent visits to our meeting place. He was always very welcome and had interesting things to say to the boys. He would end his talk by saying he wanted to shake hands, the left hand of course, with everyone present and to remind them that he had shaken hands with Baden Powell, the founder, and world chief scout, so they were shaking hands with someone who had shaken hands with B.P. that should make their day. Some would make fun of this but nevertheless B.P. was held in very high esteem by every worthy scout, he had been dead for about 20 years by this time. Lady Baden Powell was still alive and working with the sister movement.

Almost a year had passed and my warrant certificate had still not come through. I spoke to the Group Scoutmaster who told me he had filled in his part of it and passed it on, as far as he knew the Kirk Session had approved the appointment. I then went to the District Commissioner who had expressed surprise at not receiving the form, hearing that I was being appointed scoutmaster. The focus of my attention was then on the minister. I went along to see him and explained the situation. He looked at me straight in the face and said, 'Well where is it'?. Now on the window shelf of his office there was a pile of papers about 6 or 7 inches high, I was bold enough to suggest to him, could it be amongst these. 'Well let's see', he said taking the pile off the shelf and onto his desk. Going through the papers one by one, low and behold there it was waiting for his signature, this he did and handed it to me. There was another one from the cub mistress also awaiting his attention.

As far as the District Commissioner was concerned I had words with him regarding warranted scouters. It is quite clear from the Policy Organisation and Rules of the Boy Scout Movement, if a warrant is issued to an individual he must be active in the capacity for which the warrant is issued. It is also in accordance with the scout law. When I was doing P.T.C. we had a talk from a County Commissioner who said that the first scout law was not first because one of the ten had to be first, but it was first because it was the most important law. It says, 'A Scouts Honour is to be Trusted', that is if a scout says he will do a task he will do it there is no question of him not doing it. Boy Scouts after all are not scouts because they go camping, anyone can go camping, they are scouts because they abide by the law. Now I know it was not strictly my responsibility and the D.C. had other things on his mind, he did not want to lose men who could be of service to the movement, but I felt it was too important a matter to gloss over. One year the Scoutmasters were asked to fill in the census forms themselves, I was then able to give an accurate assessment of the situation and put down only those who were active. I felt that truth and accuracy were important in this matter.

It is hard to know why men in authority behave in the way they do but I was feeling a bit despondent. Baden Powell said in one of his books if a man loses his enthusiasm for running a scout troop he should give it up, well I was beginning to lose mine. I think it is good advice, nothing can be achieved without enthusiasm, if you do a job with a grudge you will never make a success of it. There are many blessings come your way in being of service to the community, but I was feeling at this time a sense of frustration and something had to be done. I left home and took up digs where about 10 or 12 young men were already living, left the church and gave up my position in the scouts. It was, I suppose a dramatic move, the new group scoutmaster was astonished

19

when I told him of my decision. The new minister pleaded with me not to go, saying no one should leave the church within one year of his calling. The new D.C. came to my house asking me to stay on but my mind was made up. On my last evening with the troop there was tears in the boys eyes but none of this would change my mind. There was some irresistible force at work, there was no turning back, but the story does not quite end there. While in the digs a group of boys decided to visit Glen Shee and the ski slopes. I went with them. A few days before we left I read in the paper that the Chief Scout was going to visit Glen Shee on the same day, however, it never occurred to me that I would see him but after we parked our car and was walking towards the slopes there he was walking in the same direction we were almost shoulder to shoulder. It was Sir Charles McLean at the time. Was this an opportunity to take my grievances to the very top. Another time he stood right in front of me, I noticed that one of his stockings was half way down his leg, all I had to do was to tap him on the shoulder and engage him in conversation. But the opportunity passed and it has always been a source of regret to me that I let this heaven sent chance pass by. It may have been a storm in a teacup but looking back now if you do not act when the opportunity presents itself then it never occurs again. Since I left the scouts I have had no contact with them whatsoever not even going to the Gang Show which is presented each year in our city. However I have much to thank the Boy Scouts for, Baden Powell was one of my heroes as a youth. His books Scouting for Boys and Rovering to Success are two of the finest books for young men to read. Yes there were good times and bad times but as the years roll by only the good times remain in memory and I will say this, that if you spend one week or more away from the town or city in the country under canvas not knowing what is going on in the world, no newspapers or wireless or TV, doing only what you have to do to live comfortably and free time in wide games and fun, you come home thoroughly refreshed, stronger in mind and spirit, spiritually uplifted and altogether a more complete person.

While I was with the scouts I was studying full time at the Heriot Watt College, a course in Mechanical Engineering. I did not pass the final exam and ended up with the equivalent of the Ordinary National Certificate in Mechanical Engineering. The complete course would have given me the Higher National Certificate. After finishing College I was given a job at the Rolls Royce, Hillington Factory in Glasgow. It was interesting working on modifications to jet engines but I missed the scouts. Although I was coming through to Edinburgh every weekend, I found trying to live in two places at the one time very unsettling so after one year and on holiday I called on a Marine Engineering firm in the city. They gave me a job as a clerk in the drawing office. It was not such an interesting job and it was less pay but I thought it was a worthwhile sacrifice to make so that I could pursue my interest in the Boy Scout Movement. Eventually when the firm heard I had my O.N.C. Certificate, I was put on the drawing board and so I became a draughtsman. Drawing was no trouble to me and I always liked drawing even from an early stage. I first worked on enquiries for steering gears then on to production drawings for stabilisers and then on to catapults. The work was interesting but I never saw the final product either in the factory or the ship. I felt if I could have gone just once on a sea trial of one of these products it would have sufficed, but it was not to be.

The boys I lived with boozed rather more than I liked. They had frequent parties and we were all supposed to put something into the kitty. I put a lot more in than I drank and so it became clear I was only helping others to get drunk. It was really not my scene and so I looked for another organisation to join and so I became a member of the Young Mens Christian Association, I was the only one in the house to join. The year was 1961 and I was 33 years of age. The next few years for recreation I had three or four groups of friends. First there was the ones I lived with whose main source of enjoyment was nights in the pub. They were a bright lot but they never aspired to anything other than that their main topic of conversation being the fortunes or misfortunes of their home football team. We pretended to be some kind of religious order and referred to each other as brother. We never went very far except one visit to Glen Shee. Then there was my friends at work, mainly unmarried outdoor types whose interests were visits to the Highlands of Scotland a nice change for us tied to the office all week. I also joined the works camera club which gave me a chance to use my camera on those journeys north. Then there was my friends in the YMCA. I was asked to join what was called the Y's Mens Club the service club of the YMCA. I also, through a member friend, joined the

21

drama club and enjoyed very much rehearsing and presenting plays in the theatre attached to the building. Two holidays abroad were one to Switzerland, just two of us, all the way there and back in a Morris Mini, and one to Ireland, four of us in my Rover car one of the most carefree, enjoyable and certainly cheapest holidays I ever spent. I should have mentioned during my time with the scouts I went with a District Troop to Denmark cycling round that lovely country for one week and spending the second week in wonderful Copenhagen. In my second set of digs there was only two of us and we decided to spend one week on the Norfolk Broads living and piloting a two berth cruiser and tasting the delights of Great Yarmouth. My fourth set of friends were those in the church although I only saw them mainly on Sunday. I was called as a Sunday School Teacher this was in my second church close to where I was staying. I was also ordained an elder in this church but more of that later. So life was interesting and it helped to beat the dreary scene at work.

A lady reading over the manuscript of this book could not understand as she put it, 'The underlying problems that led to your withdrawal from the scout movement'. That sent me thinking. I was now in my thirties and still living at home although I had been away on National Service for two years and had studied and worked in Glasgow for almost the same time. There was always an undercurrent of dissension among the scouters in the District plenty of criticism by young men feeling they were not receiving the support they would expect from those in higher rank. Every time we got into a huddle after a meeting out would come the grumbles, somebody not doing this, or that, "Well I am leaving' and so on. Scouters are taking on a responsible job and they do need the full hearted support of their leaders. Was the delay in my Warrent not going through simply a case of forgetfullness or was their some doubt as to my suitability for the job? It played on my mind. The older generation must have full confidence in the younger if they want them to respond. I am well aware that receiving a warrent does not automatically make one a super scoutmaster but it undermines one's confidence when the proper procedures are not being followed through and the question remains unanswered, why. Was it simply forgetfullness or was there some other underlying reason. I spoke to the Cub Mistress about the delay in her warrent coming through she merely shrugged her shoulder and seemed to adopt the attitude, they are a pretty dim lot up there anyway. Shortly afterwards she married. Running the scouts is a voluntary job it pays no money I had to think of my future job, home etc. I feel however the main reason was I wanted to get away from home. By this time there was a new group scoutmaster, new minister and new District Commissioner but all that made no difference The new D. C. came to my home asking me to stay on, I said no. It was time to try something new, broaden my horizons. 'When I see young boys now a days at 18 or 20 leaving home to live in digs I feel now that is what I should have done. It gives one a sense of independence and an opportunity to make ones own way in the world away from the influence of parents.

Destination Denmark

On our Leith Scout District's visit to Denmark, we teamed up with another Danish Scout Troop and cycled round the country with them on a week long trip.

On our arrival in Copenhagen, wearing our kilts and reaching our base, some of us had to go into town for an errand, I can t remember the reason why. So without changing, off we went cycling down the wrong side of the road, in a strange city and when coming to a junction I did something wrong. The traffic policemen all carry truncheons and spin them in their hand to indicate the traffic can move on. Where I made the mistake I don't know to this day, but the policeman gripped my arm with such strength I thought he would break it; they seem to exercise more authority than our policeman over here. However, on the way back my cycle wheel got caught in the tram track, not an unusual occurrence at home either, off I came with a tumble, landing on the road and hanging on to my kilt, trying to keep it up and not let my country down.

The Danish scouts camp differently from us. As most of the country is under cultivation the only camping ground is in wooded areas. Now,we were taught in Scotland never to pitch a tent near trees in case one fell during the night causing injury or worse, but in Denmark there is no alternative. We learned that many Danish scouts go camping in Norway where there is much more space. So camped in this wood we started to light a fire in the usual way but were told the Danish scouts do not use paper, instead small twigs are gathered together the size of matchsticks, or smaller, made into a cone shape on the ground and set alight. Larger pieces are then fed to the fire as it grows large enough to cook on. Denmark gets less rain than we do so drier wood is more readily available. As in our country the weather prevails from the west.

Our scoutmaster host was constantly looking at the sky to determine the weather and one occasion while setting up camp he stood some way off looking westwards, when our scoutmaster called out. 'Is it going to rain?' He turned his face towards us, his dark eyes looked darker and in a deep voice replied, 'I SINK SUNDER.'

On one occasion we camped in the garden on a well kept lawn of a farmer's cottage and we scouters were entertained to lunch by the farmer and his wife and two young girls, one, I think, was the daughter. Conversation was spasmodic, they using what English they had, we using what little Danish we had picked up. When the meal was over coffee was served and topped up with the request, 'Mere caffe?' And we would reply "Ikke mere caffe tak". The only Danish I can remember from the visit.

Denmark is in three parts; Zealand, Funen and Jutland. A ferry takes you from Zealand to Funen and to the town of Odence, the birth place of Hans Christian Anderson. He was the son of a shoemaker and his fairy tales enchanted the world and have been translated into over 100 languages. We visited the house traditionally believed to be his birth place which has been turned into a fascinating memorial, illustrating his life through letters and other memorabilia. From Funen a bridge takes you across to Jutland, the only part of Denmark which is attached to the continent of Europe, and the we travelled north to Arhus. We were fascinated by what is called Dem gamle By (The old town) an open air museum of over 60 half-timbered houses and shops. Walking in the town square was like stepping back in time and the various town offices with names on the door like the 'The Town Clerk, Provost etc. I had never seen anything like this before. From Arhus we travelled on the overnight ferry back to Copenhagen.

Our second week was spent in wonderful Copenhagen and one of the wonderful things in the centre of the city is the Tyvoli Gardens, a giant fun park for old and young. Included in this park is the Concert Hall providing classical music for all to hear. It is not necessary to sit through a one and a half to two hour programme, but entering and exiting is allowed between movements, so you only need to sit for the most fifteen to twenty minutes. It was there I became converted to classical music. The orchestra was spread out along the stage like a cinemascope movie and of course the acoustics were excellent. I can't now remember any of the pieces played, I can only remember the music filled my soul and kept repeating in my head over and over again, the clarity of the sound, every instrument could be heard. I was converted from then on. Outside old and young were enjoying the fun of the fair with much bustle and screams, but none of this was heard inside the auditorium. You could look into the building from outside through two glass screens and see the orchestra and conductor performing, but no sound was heard

The Gardens had one of the best scenic railways I have ever been on. It seemed to be full of dark tunnels and when you entered you had that sinking feeling as the carriage dropped steeply until you emerged and levelled off in daylight at the other end.

One of the country's great natural features is the complexity of its coastline providing sheltered waters for boating, bathing, fishing etc. Among the stirring sights of summer is the fluttering of a myriad colourful sails as the regattas take place round the islands. Our contribution to the seascape was the ferry boat, without sails, taking us back to Scotland.

We had good weather most of the time and our knees became sunburnt as we cycled along the level roads and our shorts rubbing against the effected parts added to our discomfort. But an enjoyable holiday nevertheless.

CHAPTER 3

Serving the Nation

Before I leave my younger years, I should say something about my two years National Service. When I left school at 15 I carried on working in my father's greengrocers shop. I always helped out after school hours. In my last summer school holidays I worked for six weeks in a market garden where my father bought fruit and vegetables. I earned 14 shillings a week, the equivalent now of less than 75p. I did not like it much. My father thought of me as a commercial traveller and arranged an interview with a wholesaler whom he dealt with but I made a hopeless mess of the interview and it came to nothing. I remember saying to my father once I would like to be an engineer, he shook his head and said, 'oh that's a dirty job'! So I worked on at the shop until my 18th birthday when my call-up papers arrived. I did six weeks army training at Dreghorn just outside Edinburgh. During our time there we were put through various tests to see what we would be best suited for. I thought I did well at assembling parts and made a request for the engineers or service corps, but they were full up. I had no engineering experience I was told and I had not done enough driving for the service corps. During the interview they discovered I was in the scouts and I had my Ambulance badge, they needed men for the Royal Army Medical Corps so that's where I was going. One wondered why they put you through the tests in the first place. The Ambulance badge was the most important badge in the scouts you wore it on both sleeves and at the top of all others. A group of us destined for this branch of the army met together and one chap was heard saying, 'It's a cushy job, no spit and polish, no army drill, no rifles (I liked firing the rifle) wear soft shoes', etc. No I did not like it, but off we went way down south to Aldershot and to Boyce Barracks near a town called Fleet. It was hot, very hot during June, July of that year. They kept us in the Barracks for a whole week before letting us out to improve our homing instincts, I suppose, and for the first time and the only time in my life I was homesick. It may have been because we were confined to barracks and assigned to various humdrum duties like cleaning the greasy pots, pans and trays in the kitchen. But when we were freed and able to walk down the country roads, past hedgerows, I began to feel better. Well six weeks at Boyce learning about the human anatomy, it wasn't too difficult — much I already knew. A nursing sister, taking the class one day, embarrassed the boys by asking the question, 'Where is the end of the alimentary canal'. There was a short pause before one student was inspired to give the correct answer. My next posting was to Birmingham to Northfield on the Bristol Road, near the Austin car factory and a psychiatric hospital. I did no medical work whatsoever the thirteen months I was in Northfield. At first in the sergeant's mess to clear up the mess which was in an awful mess after the parties the night before which was every night, and then to the quarter master store to make up the supplies ordered by the wards and units and have them delivered each day. This was a nine to five job unlike the sergeants mess which meant I had company on my time off. We spent summer nights on the Licky Hills jaunts into town and evenings in the pubs. The English pubs are jolly with usually a piano playing to add to the atmosphere. The patients in hospital were usually under observation for nervous disorder, shell shock cases and lives broken by the ravages of war. Some would end up in mental institutions, others would obtain their discharge. Patients could come and go as they pleased except for one ward known as Charlie ward where patients were locked in. I was glad to leave Birmingham after thirteen months to be posted on trooping. I did not know what it meant when I was told but due to a clerical error four of us arrived in Colchester and then sent on to Northampton to a small hospital unit. I remember it was Guy Fawkes night and we could see many fires burning from the train as we travelled in the dark. I was ten days in Northampton and never saw the place in daylight. Our eventual destination was Southampton to await a posting on a troop ship to man the hospital unit on board so I was to become a sailor for the last six months of my two years service. Many will recall that the winter of 1947/48 was one of the coldest on record. We were billeted in a transit camp which was a camp used usually for one night as soldiers moved from ship to shore before moving on, and, of course, when troops were going abroad. The huts therefore were very scantily built and had one fire in the very centre to keep 20 on so boys warm. We were given a ration of coke which was to last one week but was used up in two days. We spent a lot of time looking for additional supplies of fuel anything that would burn, wooden lavatory seats were used in the mens search for warmth. Fortunately there was a Naafi Club in town and we spent a lot of time there staying as late as we could before going home. I had so many clothes on top of me in bed I could feel the weight more than the warmth from them. Well home for Christmas and New Year and on my return a posting on the good ship Aurndel Castle. It was a bad night when we left Southampton Docks moved out into the Solent and into the English Channel with fog, a rough sea and the ship's siren blowing at regular intervals. We were a happy group on board comprising a doctor, a quartermaster, sergeant dispenser and four nursing orderlies. Two orderlies were posted in the hospital, one in the kitchen, and one in the M. I. Room. Anyone who was sick reported first to the M. I. room. (I think it meant Medical Information). Late on in the evening we were told a man had taken an epileptic fit in one of the holds, so off we went with a straight jacket and bending our backs beneath the hammocks got hold of the patient and took him to the ward. He was not struggling but more unconscious and when moved on to the bed just lay there. We all looked at him and then I was assigned to night shift to keep an eye on him, this was my introduction to medical service. I asked the Scot's doctor what should I do if he takes a fit during the night, 'Oh just come and get me, my cabin is two decks above', he replied. Well that was comforting for me and the patient to know. The man opened his eyes in the early hours of the morning and looked upon the world as if he had

On the 'Georgic'. The author is second from the right.

seen it for the first time and then went to sleep again. We did not have patients in the ward every night so I did not know if I would be on duty or not which sort of upset my sleeping pattern. The quartermaster who was in charge of the team was from South Africa and a very talkative person. We would all gather together of an evening and listen to him and the doctor having a discourse and discussion on almost every subject under the sun, the experience of the older man proving too much for the young doctor who had to eat humble pie to his junior officer on numerous occasions. Ten days took us into Port Said at the entrance to the Suez Canal. It was warm on deck in the night air and everything was of a hustle and bustle with little boats going to and fro and sounding their horns, some crammed with wares mainly of the leather variety. The following morning we went ashore and I could feel the sun very hot on my back. It was difficult to pass shops without the owner or somebody beckoning you in with the remark, 'No charge for look round'. So we had a look round many shops and that was about all we could do because us soldiers did not have that much money. The owners did not like us asking the price of goods. One of them explained 'you ask for an article, you examine the article, when you decide, then you ask the price'. However one of our number, knowing this was particularly provocative in one shop asking the price of every article much to the annoyance of the owner. The little dark man stood next to me looking at the soldier and shaking his head. He spoke and said 'Tell me is that man an Englishman?', I replied in the affirmative, he shook his head again an said 'Are you an Englishman?', I replied that I was a Scotsman 'Ah', he said 'You the real McKay'. It was another Scotsman, Johnnie Walker, that bade us farewell as we passed the famous sign advertising Scotch whisky at the entrance to the harbour. After a three week journey we were back in Southampton. My next ship was the Empress of Scotland, formally the Empress of Japan but the name was changed when Japan entered the war. She was a luxury liner and we four had a large cabin to ourselves with our own washing and toilet facilities. She was fast at 21 knots passing everything at sea. We had a fairly quiet time on board I can't think of anything of note that took place. A few patients in hospital it was a lazy cruise to the Middle East and back a three week's trip. Rough weather kept us outside Malta harbour for a day and the following morning through the port hole I saw a tug coming towards the ship, that is I saw it when it was on the crest of a wave but it completely disappeared when it was in the trough. Our entrance to the harbour was precarious as a heavy swell could be seen to carry the ship forward while negotiating the narrow entrance. My next ship was the 'Georgic' a sister ship to the Cunard White Star 'Britannic'. She was bombed and burnt out at Suez in the early days of the war, towed to India, and fitted out as a troop ship. She became the largest British troop ship at sea. Bunks were fitted throughout, there were no hammocks but she had no luxury. Many of the steel plates were buckled both inside and out with the extreme heat of the fire, she was painted grey all over and had one squat funnel slightly aft of amidships. She was kept at a speed of 17 knots. If things had been quiet in the first two ships things were to liven up on the Georgic. I did two trips on her, one three week trip to the Middle East and after a quick turn around in Liverpool a six week trip to East Africa and back.

Our team this time had grown to two doctors, two nurses, a chemist, and four orderlies. I was assigned to the M I. room. We had a large contingent of troops on board all destined for the Middle East and all required inoculation. It was done efficiently and orderly by the troops standing in line one behind the other sleeves rolled up as far as they could go hands on hip. The orderly would give the upper arm a clean with antiseptic and cotton wool, the doctor would then administer the jag. The second orderly applied a patch to the pin prick and that was that, the soldier left to roll down his sleeve and move on. The Second Lieutenants, however, the young men on the first rung of the commissioned officer's ladder, had to be given special treatment. Asked to attend the M. I. room at a specific time all five arrived together in great anticipation as to what would happen to them. The doctor began to explain the procedure and at one point one of them fainted and fell a heap on the floor, another wobbled at the knees and just managed to sit himself on a chair, the others went deadly white but were able to stay on their feet. We then gave the jag in the appropriate place and breathed a sigh of belief when it was all over. F.F.I. were also carried out (Free From Infection). The men exposed themselves to the doctor and if he thought they were affected they were given a small tube of white cream and a dab of cotton wool but no instructions as to how it should be applied. A man reported sick the following day showing what looked like three over ripe tomatoes hanging from his groin. The doctor's remark 'good gracious' was a bit of an understatement. What the cure was, if the doctor knew, I never found out, we only hoped it would have no permanent affect on his manhood. We carried out lots of minor operations such as tooth extraction, insertions to release poison, splints or plaster to deal with minor accidents. The trouble was sometimes the patients would come round before the operation was over and it was impossible to give a second jag. One chap having poison removed from his upper leg and while he was being bandaged asked the doctor if it was over 'Not quite but almost' was the reply he got. 'Good', he said 'The wife will be pleased'. A little Irishman came into the M.I. room with what looked liked a piece of rag hanging from his hand, it was what was left of his thumb after allowing a vertical port hole window to fall on it. He was given an anaesthetic and the doctor was in the process of putting his thumb together again when the patient came round. It became apparent he had a dislike of army officers and the doctor was in uniform. 'Are you an officer', he would say. There was no reply. 'Let me get at him'. He showed tremendous strength and it took the three of

Crossing the 'Line'

us present to hold him down to prevent the doctor getting hurt and perhaps needing an operation himself. I think the worst case of ingratitude
I have ever come across. On this trip we called in at Haifi to take on
board about 40 patients on an over night journey to Port Said. They
were patients mainly with shot gun injuries. One chap had a bullet
wound in his stomach and the bullet had been removed from his back
so he had two wounds to dress. He was able to give me instructions as
to how it should be done so I was able to assist causing him as little discomfort as possible. Another man had the whole of his stomach wall
removed so that you could see everything inside. There was an issue
from him and you no sooner had him dressed when he was calling to
have it attended to again. How he was expected to live I just do not
know. I kept looking out of the port hole during the night for Port Said
knowing we could be discharging the patients there. We were very tired
having been up all day and all night. Most of the contingent disem-
barked at Port Said and we had very few on board as we made our way
down the Suez Canal. There should always be someone in attendance at
the M. I. room for obvious reasons, illness can happen at any time and

accidents too. Things were very quiet as we made our way down the canal so I thought I would take a stroll round the ship. Making my way to the open deck, there was nobody about, I took a walk down the promenade deck leaning on the rail if it was not too hot, watching the after wave from the ship moving slowly and steadily along. I then made my way down to the hospital deck and looking along the corridor I could see the door of the M.I. room open. I was sure I closed it when I left. It was hot, the heat from the engine adding to the heat of the day as I moved along the corridor, when I looked inside the room I could not believe my eyes. Everybody was there except me who should have been there and five or six soldiers some lying some sitting and the staff trying to remove wooden splinters from their faces and eyes. I helped out as best I could. The two men with damaged eyes were bandaged and put into the ward, the others left badly shaken. What had happened I learned later was that a group of soldiers were standing talking, rifles slung over their shoulders pointing downward and one went off, the bullet hitting the wooden deck threw wooden chips into the faces and eyes of those standing about. I had heard or seen nothing of this during my walk about. I expected to be severely reprimanded for my absence but nothing was said and I continued at my post. After Suez our next call was at Port Sudan half way down the Red Sea. I was in the cabin and thought I heard voices outside. Looking out I saw a tug pulling a large platform or barge on which goods from the ship were to be set down. The natives were being thrown cigarettes from the men on board and there was a mad scramble for them all in good fun. They stuck the cigarettes in their hair where I learned later they kept many articles, they were Fuzzie Wozzies with hair on their heads like crow's nests. We were able to get ashore for a short time at Aden and trample on 'The barren rocks of Aden' to quote a Scottish pipe tune, very dry and completely lacking in moisture. In the Indian Ocean it was cooler as we made our way south over the 'line' to Mombassa. The usual celebrations as subjects were brought before King Neptune tried, sentenced and punished (Pasted) for entering his kingdom, then a day's sailing to enter Kilindinny Docks and anchored offshore. We did get one day on dry land to set foot in Kenya and examine life in Mombassa. Veiled women were in evidence as we walked down the main street and then to a restaurant to enjoy the best mixed grill I think I have ever had, served up by waiters in white with big smiles and teeth to match. As soon as there were people aboard ship we had to be on duty so after a week's stay and only one day ashore we began our return journey. Moving out into the Indian Ocean it was rough, the ship moved about a bit and we had people asking for sea sick tablets. We had a large contingent of Polish emigrants on board presumably going back to Poland having been evacuated during the war. They were of all ages. I remember twin girls in their teens, inseparable until one was ill with malaria and had to enter hospital, even then the other sat outside the ward door the closest she could get to her sister. We did have sea sick pills in a small bottle marked poison kept locked in a cupboard, they were not to be given out without instructions from the doctor. I can only remember once a lady being given pill from the poison bottle, as far as I know she survived. If therefore people said they were sick they were given one aspro, it would not cure headaches but it had a marvellous effect in curing sea sickness but I think the cure was more physiological than real. After a day and a half out a group of immigrants came to us indicating we were to go with them, so we did, to the aft of the ship then down stairs, down and down we went I had no idea the ship went so far down to what looked like a bundle of laundry lying in a comer of the deck. Looking under this we discovered a lady in a very distressed condition, red in the face and perspiring freely. She was a rather big lady and I think had crawled into this corner to die, sea sickness can have this affect on people. Well we had to get her out and up on deck Taking an arm each and getting others to help we got her to the foot of the stairs, some pushed, some pulled, others shouted encouragement, she protested but we eventually got her up all these steps we had come down. Sitting her on deck in the open we left her there. Later in the afternoon we called back to see if she was all right, there were ladies sitting on the bench but we could not recognise her, well not at first, a new summer dress on and a big smile on her face quite unrecognisable from the lady we knew in the morning, what a difference a little fresh air and sunshine had made.

Late one night, we entered the Red Sea, a strong wind was blowing and we were bare to the waist to feel the warm air on our chests. News came through that a mental patient had escaped from the ward and we had to search the ship for him. It proved to be a bit of a pantomime as so many soldiers had opted to sleep on deck, it being too warm below. In the dark we tripped over bodies, fell over them, took many a tumble ourselves before the patient showed up having just taken a walk around the ship and not intending to throw himself overboard.

It would be my fifth time in Port Said and last time. We were not allowed ashore as relations between ourselves and the Egyptians were deteriorating. A few years on Nasser nationalised the Suez Canal which resulted in its closure due to the war and the resignation of the British Prime Minister Sir Anthony Eden. I remember being at a scout camp when this news filtered through to us. I enjoyed my stint in the 'Navy', every turn of the ship's screw is taking you to new places on the way out and every turn of the screw is taking you nearer home on the way back. The big ship lumbered and cork-screwed crossing the Bay of Biscay as a heavy swell came in from the Atlantic and then we were home. On the return journey the quartermaster sergeant asked me into his office, he wanted to promote me to a three star private the only hint of promotion I received in the two years, but as I was being demobbed when I got back it was not pursued and so I left the army as I joined it as a private soldier doing his duty for his country and to this day has not forgotten his army number 14181931 Sir!

CHAPTER 4

Family History

In the summer of 1948 I was demobbed. For a holiday, my mother, brother and myself went up to the Shetland Islands. The St. Clair, a much smaller boat than the Georgic, seemed to bob and down on the water like a cork on its way to the islands, I could not get used to the motion. I have never been sea sick but I came near to it then, with a splitting headache and unsteady gait as I went ashore at the end of the journey. However, the discomfort soon passed as we made our way north to visit our friends and relatives on those beautiful islands. Why the Shetland Islands? Well now I would like to write a little of my family genealogy.

I was born in Edinburgh on the 30th day of May 1928, christened Gilbert Robert Williamson after my grandfather on my father's side whom I never met. My father was born and brought up in the Shetland Islands and left there as a young man to seek fame and fortune in the south. There were seven in the family altogether, the mother's name being Barbara Charlotte Williamson she had the same surname, they were in fact cousins. They were married in Lerwick on 2nd December 1879 and lived on the north of the second largest island in the group called Yell. My grandfather lived as a crofter/fisherman and raised his

'Newhouse' where my father grew up as a child

'Newhouse' with the upper extension built on. My Aunt Johan at the door of the new porch with 'Fan' the dog

family in 'Newhouse' Midbrake, Cullivoe, Yell, Shetland. My father was the second last in the family born on the 1st April 1893 and christened John Gray Williamson. He and his older brother William born on 23rd May 1888 were the only two to leave Shetland to work and raise their families in Scotland's capital city Edinburgh. So Shetland played a big part in our lives going on holiday there every second year for three weeks while we were children, during the thirties. Holidays were described as 'going home'. I did know my grandmother always dressed in black from her head to her toes. She kept us at a distance, I don't remember being lifted by her or being sat on her knee but then we may have been too big for that or she may have been too frail, but one incident I do remember. My father did not stay the three weeks but came up on the last week only. On this occasion he was very well dressed on arrival at the house. hat, shoulder hanging raincoat, suit and fine shoes, he really looked as if he had made his fortune and was coming home to let them see. His mother was delighted and pride showed in her face as she met her son half way and continued to pat him on the shoulder as she walked him back to the house.

My father with his mother, Ann and I in Shetland

The seven members of the family were as follows: Agnes born 31~ December 1882; Johan born 4th January 1884; Gilbert born 3rd April 1886; William born 23rd May 1888; Peter Moat Sandison born 7th February 1891; John Gray born 1st April 1893; Johan Jessie born 21st March 1896.

As the first Johan died in infancy (7 years) the next daughter born was given the same name but she had Jessie added to it. The ones I knew apart from my father were William and Peter, my uncles and Johan, my aunt. Gilbert married a Jessie Leask on the 24th August 1915 in Lerwick they had two daughters Kathleen and Anna. However Gilbert died in 1932 and Jessie married again a Lowrie Henry. When we went on holiday we stayed in Newhouse with Peter and Johan and Kathleen. The two girls did not take to their stepfather and both wanted to stay with their uncle and aunt who they had been staying with fol-lowing the bereavement. The younger girl however was persuaded to return home, Kathleen stayed on with her uncle and aunt. So that was the company we kept when we went 'home', Jessie's house was just a short distance from Newhouse.

I have many memories of those holidays in Shetland and many inci-dents that remain firmly in my mind, too numerous to mention here. I would like however to go back even further to my grandparents. Gilbert Robert's father was Peter John Williamson born in 1827. He married a Barbara Sinclair on 19th February 1851. Gilbert Robert was born on 4th April 1854 and was married as has been said on 2nd December 1879. Turning now to the other side Barbara Charlotte's father was William John Williamson he was born in 1812 and married an Agnes Moar on the 19th July 1845. Barbara Charlotte was born on 20th 1851. In 1881 a terrible tragedy took place known as the Gloup Fishing Disaster. Gloup is a small community off the north tip of Yell. I had known of this tragedy of course but did not know the extent to which my family were involved until I did some research. As the hundredth anniversary of this event approached a committee was formed whose aim was to erect a memorial near the site of the Gloup fishing station to commemorate this tragic event. A booklet published on the occasion says 'on the night of 20/21st July 1881, a sudden and terrible storm caught the 'haal' fisherman of Shetland at sea. Ten boats containing fifty-eight men, were lost, leaving thirty-four widows and eighty-five children in destitution'. Gilbert and Barbara, only a year and a half married and as yet no family lost both their fathers, Peter aged 53 and William aged 69 in this tragedy, bodies lost without trace. Laurence Williamson a brother to William was also lost. This tragedy has vibrated ever since to move people not to forget this event such as the Memorial Committee and roughly ten years after that a Cantata was written and performed in the Clickimin Centre in September 1992. Music written by David Bard and titled 'Beyond the Far Haaf'. The Lerwick performance was covered in the Shetland Times newspaper which said:- 'The work was based on the tragic tale of the Gloup fishing disaster of 1881 when 58 men from the community were drowned at sea in their sixareens when a violent storm blew up out of a clear sky, . . . for the civility of the glittering evening the cantata fully brought home the gravity, the emotion and the far-reaching effects of such a disaster . . . The work was shocking, stimulating, griping and powerful, and at the end of the orchestra's excellent rendering there were even one or two wiping away a tear". The poem printed in the booklet was said to have been published shortly after the event in the Shetland Times newspaper. The poem is written in English and 'is the work of an unknown poet who would appear to have been a native of North Yell'. It is not mentioned in the Booklet but I was told that the non de plume given was W.W. and the last time I was in Shetland some people said it might have been my uncle William Williamson. Well now my uncle was born in 1888 and if the poem was written shortly after the event in 1881 it could not have been him. But the poem is written in English and therefore it could have been someone like my uncle exiled in the 'south' all his working life. I have written to the Shetland archives to ascertain the exact date when the poem was published because it all hinges on this. (*See poem at the back of the book.*)

I knew my Uncle of course and have wondered ever since did he have any literary talent. The families met periodically sometimes in our house in the north of the city and sometimes in theirs in the south. On one occasion we went skating on the Union Canal it being frozen on a particularly hard winter the canal running close to my Uncle's house at Craiglochart. The children were Annie and Bertie our cousins, and good times we had with them. Bertie was a few years older than me and a great hero of mine, a great extrovert and full of fun. But more often my uncle would come down to our house on his own, his visits unannounced and sometimes my parents were not in. When I grew older I felt I should entertain him since he had come a long way, so what does an Uncle ask his nephew, inevitably it is, 'what are you doing at school?' At one time I told him we were studying Dickens novel Pickwick Papers in the English class. "Oh"! he said "I have read that book" and then he began to remember parts of it and would laugh heartily at the people in it saying that many of the characters in the book reminded him of people in Shetland. Dickens novel is of course about the weird and wonderful characters occupying the London scene but Shetland too has its fair share of weird and wonderful characters. Another time asking the same question I told him I was studying the French language. Oh! he replied I like reading books in French. I thought, he's a clever fellow who can read books in French. He then asked me what does Qui mean in French. he pronounced it Oi! I replied that it means Yes. Oh is that what it means he said. How he was able to read French and not know what Oi! meant I do not know. So that is the extent of my knowledge of my uncle's literary skills.

When the brothers did get together there were three things they would talk about, first it was Shetland, what was new on the islands, and recalling old times my uncle would laugh heartily remembering his youthful days and exploits with the 'boys'. Next it was business, both had similar types of business, my uncle a grocer and my father a greengrocer being at opposite ends of the town there was no rivalry there. My father visited the fruit market every day my uncle only now and again. Speaking to a salesman from the fruit market one day after my uncle had died, he knew both men, and referred to my uncle as 'Cherry' this because of his ruddy red cheeks and the fact he was always laughing. The third topic of conversation was politics and there the amicable relations came to an end. Both had opposite views on every subject discussed and the argument became very heated at times. If the wives were present they would never enter the argument but sit there with long faces and if anything try to introduce a new topic into the conversation to steer the men away from their confrontation.

My father and uncle were very different men. Of the four brothers in three you could detect a relationship but William was very different in appearance. Serious men I would say although I never knew my Uncle

First ten-day leave from the army

My sister and I with our grandfather

*With our cousins Anna and Kathleen
in Shetland*

My parents on honeymoon in Moffat

Gilbert but William was the complete extrovert. He seemed also to have passed this on to his son Bertie but Annie his older daughter was more of a serious nature. It is said that families can be split down the middle some are serious and others are happy-go-lucky. In our family I'm the serious one but my younger sister and brother are happy-go-lucky. It was Robert Burns, the Scottish poet, in his study of men came also to this conclusion that all men belong to either one category or the other. Willie used to stammer in his speech but it was not too noticeable but Peter who lived in Shetland was much worse. Peter was a likable person who liked company and liked to talk and some thought it was unfortunates that he should be handicapped in this way. He seemed almost to tire himself out trying to overcome his speech impediment. Our holidays with Uncle Peter, Aunt Johan and Kathleen held many memories for us. One trip I remember we left Leith Docks on a Monday morning on the yacht styled St Sunniva seen off by our grandfather, my mother's father, sailing out into the Forth on a beautiful day sitting on the sun deck passing Inchkeith Island and on to Aberdeen. A short stay there and then an overnight journey to Lerwick arriving in the early morning. We would then disembark and board the much smaller Earl of Zetland, to take us to Mid Yell Voe. There boarding a flit boat to the pier and then a bus journey north to Cullivoe arriving in the early afternoon. Most children enjoy Shetland the open landscape and the sense of freedom it brings. We could not wait to get outside and look around the croft to see the animals and fields. There was a beautiful beach nearby called the Sands of Breakon and that was always an attraction,

My mother when she reached her nineties used to reminiscence a lot about her childhood. She had a happy childhood born in Wardlaw Place off the Gorgie Road on 19th February 1904. The family moved house several times but she talked a lot about Beaverhall Road off Broughton Road where several members of the family lived in the same stair and others not far away. It was there that her father was prevailed upon to join St. James Church in McDonald Road. The minister the Rev. Thomas Porteous was also a member of the School Board and took a liking to James Davidson and managed to get him a job as a school janitor. So after trying various occupations James Davidson became janitor of Sciennes School in the south part of the city which meant a move for

My parents wedding in Edinburgh June 1927

The Grant Family with twelve of their thirteen children. My grandmother is the lady top centre, wearing the light-coloured dress

the family to West Newington Place. They however retained their membership of St James's and my mother talks about the long walk twice each Sunday from home to church and back again. Her mother's family the Grants made their way south from Morayshire I imagine bit by bit as they grew up, there were thirteen of them, and a house was purchased at 50A Brunswick Street off Leith Walk. This then became a convenient stopping place for rest and refreshment on the long haul each Sunday. Granny and grandad too made their way to Edinburgh to be near their grandchildren and to see them growing up. My grandad might have been called a pillar of the Kirk assuming responsibilities as Elder, Sunday School Superintendent, and Beedle. His next school was Abbeyhill School which of course brought the family nearer the Church and his last appointment was to Canongate School and to a house at 16 Jeffrey Street. On his retirement the family purchased a bungalow at Blackhall, 33 Craigcrook Avenue where he lived out the remaining 18 years of his life. He retired not only from work but also from church activities spending most of the day outside in the garden and adjoining allotment coming in some days only for his meals.

My mother left school on Friday and started work on Monday. She recalls going with her mother for an interview with a Mr Blair who owned the drapery store on South Bridge just down from the Empire Theatre. On coming away her mother said, 'You will not get the job you did not call the man 'sir'.'However, a letter arrived shortly after offering her the job. She worked there for nine years before she was married. My mother was a shop girl and loved serving customers and if she had her time over again she would go back to shop life. Later when the family was growing up she worked in my father's shop and selling fruit and vegetables was no different than selling socks and hankies to her. It was serving the public, seeing customers satisfied, pleased that she was able to help with their purchases then on to the next one.

My father, when he first left home, worked in a pub in Lerwick before coming to Edinburgh and stayed with his Aunt Mary in Annandale Street. During the first world war he spent his time coaling the fleet off Rosyth. He also worked for a time in the Shakespeare Bar in Lothian Road close to the Usher Hall. His aunt was also a member of St. James and so he went with her occasionally when time and desire permitted. My mother recalls seeing these two fine men sitting in the

Beginning my turn on earth. There are four generations in this picture — great grandmother, mother and grandmother

pew (my father and his older brother William) and was impressed by both with their fine physique and wavy hair. His first shop was in St. Mary's Street selling fruit and vegetables and he obtained a flat also in Jeffrey Street opposite where my mother stayed. He eventually had five shops whether bought or rented I do not know, all confectionery shops and I can just recall going round with him in his Morris car visiting each one. If I can remember there was one in Leith walk, one in Elm Row, Clerk Street, Dalry, and Gorgie Road. However I do not think they all showed a profit and so they were given up retaining only one in Clerk Street which he must have bought and rented out. His last shop was one he purchased new, I remember him saying for £700.0p, in Wardieburn Drive selling fruit, vegetables and confectionery and lived out his life there all during the war years retiring in 1959 at age 66.

I wish it were possible to turn the clock back and see my father serving beer behind the bar or on board ship as an ordinary seaman or to see my mother walking up the High Street in Edinburgh down South Bridge to enter the shop and serving customers behind the counter, but such things are not possible. They were married in St James Church on the 28th June 1927 and spent their honeymoon in Moffat in the border country of Scotland.

My grandmother was born in Alves, Elgin, Morayshire on the 4th May 1877 and christened Ann Grant being the fourth in line of a family of 13 children; her parents were James Grant and Catherine Anton Dunbar. Her husband was James John Davidson born in Kincardine O'Neil on 1st April 1870 being the third in a family of four his parents were William Davidson and Ann Troup so my father and grandfather shared the same birthday date 1st April. The couple had four children my mother being the eldest and the only one that married, the third child Mary died in infancy. My mother outlived both her brother Jim and sister Dorothy and was particularly upset when her sister 11 years her junior died. Jim was involved in a very serious accident a head on collision with a van while on his motor cycle. He was able to return to work but never fully recovered from his injuries. My Uncle Jim was a life long member of the Boy Scouts Association and only gave up when his health and eyesight began to fail. He was an engineer and he and I shared the same interest in motor car racing when I was young. That then is the family background.

Shetland for us as children was a see-saw in the garden, flying a kyte, fun on the beach looking for shells, climbing the cliffs (banks) bringing water from the well, carting home the peats for winter, moving the milking cow. The cow was flitted morning and evening and perhaps during the day,and on the way,might be taken to the burn for a drink. On one occasion I untethered the animal and wrapping the rope round my hand,walked in the direction of the burn. As soon as the cow smelt water it was off. What happened next can best be described as the dog taking his master for a walk. Unable to untangle the rope because of the constant pull by the animal, I was lucky to be still on my feet on reaching the waters edge.

Visits to the shop could be eventful. On one occasion a group of us began the one mile walk taking the dog along. Passing a cottage on the way,the dog took off at high speed towards the building, Looking to see what had attracted its attention a cat was seen sitting at the door and the cat seeing the dog coming in its direction ran along the front of the house up the side and then disappeared round the back. The dog kept up the chase and then the cat was seen on the roof of the house at its very apex. It ran along towards the chimney at the gable end being pursued shortly after by the dog. The cat then climbed the chimney pot,pausing momentary before sliding down and out of view. The dog then gave up the chase and joined us on the road. On our return we called into the cottage regarding the welfare of the cat and was glad to see it in the arms of its owner apparently none the worse of its experience.

During the war children were evacuated to Shetland and in the building next to ours, called the 'Haa', several evacuees stayed, so we had plenty of companions. Two old ladies also stayed there always dressed in black from head to toe. They had lived their lives in Shetland and when I was a youth I was bid to go and have conversation with them. They were very friendly and talkative but the discourse was very one way, their accents and local knowledge left me quite bemused..

Lowrie Hendry, my Aunt Jessie's second husband, could pull a face that would frighten children. His prominent cheek bone and protruding chin,but especially the eyes, cold and piercing, could scare many an adult and children did cry on eye to eye contact with him. I was coming away from the-house once when I realised one of my shoe laces was undone. I bent down to tie the lace and on straightening up there

Uncle Peter, Auntie Johan and my father. In the front row are Anna, Kathleen and Roseanna, Kathleen's daughter

From the right. Anna, her mother, Jessie, holding Roseanna, and step-father Lowrie Henrie

49

was Lowrie face to face almost eyeball to eyeball with me. I had heard or seen nothing of him until then, but I knew him too well to be scared by him. His face would then crease into a smile his eyes would soften and then he d stretch out his arm for a hand shake.

The beach nearby is called the Sands of Breakon a fine stretch of sand which you can have to yourself most times. It was here my father would lay out his fluke line across the bay. In the morning we would go to the beach and with a hooked knife draw the blade through the wet sand close to the waters edge and up would come the sand eels. We would fill the bucket and return to the house to bait the line. At low tide the line was laid out across the bay and at high tide it would be drawn in with many flounders and one or two dog fish. The dog fish were difficult to kill and my uncle would dash them against the rocks to hasten their demise. We did not eat them but fed them to the hens. You cannot get fish any fresher than in Shetland and a feed of boiled cod, home grown tatties and home made butter is a very satisfying meal.

Visiting a friend's house on one occasion I refused a glass of whisky, also a cup of tea, in exasperation he asked if I would have a glass of milk. His wife brought from the kitchen a pint glass full to the brim and I have never forgotten the rich quality of that drink its effect has lived with me ever since.

These northern isles have many attractions one being the almost perpetual light during the summer months. One evening arriving home late about a quarter to one in the morning, I looked out towards the open sea. Even in the wee small hours you can still see the other islands and the horizon (the horizon is always worth looking at in Shetland) I saw what looked like an armada of small ships making for the islands. I went into the house where some relatives were just leaving to go home. They were only gone a minute when they returned and asked us to come outside. Our eyes beheld at what looked like an invasion, and lights from two small fishing boats nearer the shore added realism to this. Bows, decks, and funnels were all in evidence but on closer inspection it turned out to be mere cloud formations on the horizon!

The dialect is somewhat different from ours, some would think almost a foreign language; rod for road and brunt for burnt. One day my mother was making fish for dinner and she asked me to go to the shop for some pepper. The shop was in the 'Haa' and as you entered the

My father with his first car. A Model T Ford

My mother with the same car

large building you had to shout 'shop' to indicate your intentions from a social visit. The lady going behind the counter asked what I wanted. "Pepper," I said. "What kind of pepper do you want?" she asked. I was not aware there was different kinds of pepper and replied any kind. "What do you want the pepper for?" she asked. "For fish," I said "We are having fish for dinner." "What way do you want to put pepper on fish?" she asked again. So the discussion continued until she eventually realised it was pepper of the salt and pepper variety and not pepper as applied to"newspepper!"

I used to like watching my uncle mowing hay with a scythe. The even rhythmic movement as he swayed from side to side always held me spell bound. To announce meal times my aunt would blow a whistle and then my uncle would lay aside the scythe and we would start climbing the hill towards the house. With the dogs by our side my uncle would stop every now and again to look back at a neatly mowed field,always a pretty sight,and the higher you got the prettier it became.

Shetland is a haven for sea birds. One day out for a walk I came across a kittiwake chick sitting on a rock, its grey and white plumage almost hid the bird from its grey setting. I sat beside the chick for a few minutes, it made little or no movement, all was peaceful for a while and then I was startled by a shriek at my ear. The mother bird protecting her young was dive bombing and being more than effective in chasing off this intruder. I was some distance away before she gave up her attacks.

Dogs and cats have a most peaceful and happy relationship in the home. In complete contrast, however, to the conditions at home all out war exists between the dogs and the neighbourhood cats. Our home boasted of two dogs and four cats. When outside it is difficult for the dogs to tell their own from the neighbours but the general idea seems to go for it anyway. A cat appears on the dyke in front of the house and the two dogs guarding the door start of in its direction. With much barking and bustle the dogs reach the cat which then arches its back in readiness no doubt having had to put up with this performance before. The dogs then sniff the cat satisfied it is one of theirs and it gets a free passage home. It is amusing to see a cat approach from the rear of the house. It peers round the corner of the building, sees the dog guarding the door, but the dog can't see it from behind. The cat then makes a bee line for the door and as it passes to go inside gives the dog a nudge as if to say 'friend'

One bright sunny September morning I sat by the banks fascinated by the heavy sea breaking on the shore. Now and again a particularly high wave followed by perhaps two others would be seen approaching and you wondered if it was safe to stand your ground or move inshore. The waves seem to be trying to destroy the banks as if some war was on between the two. Sometimes water would shoot up as if an underwater depth charge had gone off. Just a short distance from this, a loch, the water calm on the surface with little wavelets breaking on the shore in complete contrast to the turmoil going on just a stones throw away.

Shetland is a place of contrasts, the almost continuous day light in summer to the dark nights of winter. To the beautiful sunny days when the pollution free atmosphere brings out the colour of the green grass, the grey of the rocks, the dazzling white of the breakers on the shore and the Mediterranean blue of the sea, to the extreme dull drab grey of a wet misty rainy day and a stiff breeze bringing water to the eyes. From a peaceful morning when all is quiet only the call of distant sea birds breaking the silence of the day to the roar of the sea waves breaking against the banks in gale force winds accompanied by a boiling sea.

There is something quite substantial about the Shetland way of life, a great acceptance of things as they are, always a sense of humour in their conversation, liberal in outlook, all shades of opinion are expressed but none taken too seriously. If a man marries, raises a family, works all his life to provide for them, then he has reached the pinnacle that any man can reach. The simple life is what many people crave for and from time to time you hear of families turning their back on the rat race in the south and going north to buy or rent a croft on the islands. My father was always impressed when he heard of people doing this. "God will provide," was their belief,of course he never did it himself but then he found his haven in the south.

Windhouse

On one of the Shetland islands called Yell, stands a house long since unoccupied and now in a very ruinous state,but which still remains a landmark. Driving along the road running north the house can be seen on the left at the top of a rise. It is quite an elaborate building on two stories with the top windows projecting from the roof, a raised garden at the front and an archway over the entrance. There are bay windows on the side of the house and a walled garden at the rear. In its present state it looks very sinister with windows boarded up, where some planks have been removed, it reveals an inky darkness inside.

The story of the 'Mannor' is that it was built by eight men who came from the south. After it was finished seven men only returned. It was believed that the missing man was murdered by his work mates. Substance was given to this story when years later human remains were found under a stone at the rear door of the house. Whether this is true or not several residents have been unable to stay long because of peculiar noises occurring during the night. Since it has been unoccupied a light has been seen shining from one of the windows during the hours of darkness. I parked my car off the road on a beautiful afternoon, the sun shining brightly. The ground was wet due to heavy rain having fallen the night before. Watching my step to avoid the wet patches I climbed the hill and reached the raised garden at the front of the house. It was little different in appearance since I last saw it four years previously. The winter gales had removed parts of the masonry, the railings on the garden wall were missing and the archway to the garden was leaning over at an angle. One wondered how many more winter gales it would survive before finally falling to the ground. Having taken my fill of the of the front edifice, I made my way to the rear of the building. Taking another look and trying to detect changes since I last saw it I moved into the back garden which was surrounded by a wall. There plants and small trees,protected by the wall were growing wild and moving in the gentle breeze. I looked at the unkept garden and took in the silence all around, a few birds were flying passed and one felt very much away from it all.

It was then I heard a noise like the breaking branch of a tree or if something had just snapped inside the building. I tried to dismiss it from my mind, but it would not go away. Trying to behave as normal as possible and taking my time I walked down the side path to the front of the house. All sorts of things were going through my mind but something had aroused my sensitivities; I was concerned and not quite sure of my surroundings. When I eventually reached the front garden it became apparent what had aroused my feelings. A young man was walking up the steps to the front garden and carrying in his hands a

Kathleen feeding her calf on 'The Whilks'

Maggie Jean, Kathleen and her husband, Robbie

rifle. Well this explained the sound I'd heard it had been a gun shot! Wearing blue jeans and a brown polar necked jersey he walked on purposely and when we passed I uttered Hi! He returned the Hi! and walked on. Descending the garden steps I looked over my shoulder to see the man looking round the left hand corner of the house. He looked for a time and then turned to walk briskly passed the front of the house trying not to show his face, and then up the path I had just come down. I stood for a time puzzled, the encounter was over in less than a minute. Had I really seen a man or was my imagination playing tricks. I stood for a time not knowing whether to walk towards the house or away from it. After a pause I began to descend the hill, looking back occasionally to see if anyone was watching, however I saw no one. On reaching the road I leaned on the car and looked back at the house a silhouette on the skyline it looked no different than before. In a field nearby crofters were working quietly to them a perfectly normal afternoon

Later that day I mentioned the incident to some friends. They listened in mild amusement and suggested it was a student out shooting rabbits. This is a possible explanation, however the Mannor has lost its attraction for me now. When I return I will look up, recall that afternoon in memory and drive on by.

CHAPTER 5

At the Deep End

When I left home and the scouts to live in digs I felt I needed some other form of spiritual uplift. I did not leave the church but took my lines to another nearer where I was now staying. This church supported the Boys Brigade so I was not likely to be involved there so I looked for something else and joined the Y.M.C.A. The year was 1962 and I was working as a draughtsman in a local marine engineering firm. The Y.M. building was in the centre of the town and was open daily providing a varied programme for young people. I met a man there who was a member of the Y's Mens Club and also worked for the same company as I did. The Y's Mens Club was the service club of the Y.M.C.A. a group of more mature men who ran projects to help finance the Association and get new units started. Some people were amused and thought they were called the Wise Men. You could go to the Y.M. building any night of the week where there was a lounge, cafeteria, a gymnasium and a theatre there to meet friends and plan projects. Folk groups used to perform on the Saturday nights. Well I became a Y's man and was involved in a number of activities to raise funds. We were an international organisation and held conferences in Nottingham, England, which meant travelling there from time to time. I became president of the local club for one year. What I remember most about those days was my membership of the Drama Club. Now I had always admired actors and often wished I could do what they did but remembering lines I could not see me doing that. The first programme I was involved in was a three off one act plays. We had a producer called Harry who was a member of the Y.M. and a secretary of a local hostel and one time provost of a provincial town. I was given the smallest of parts that of a prison warden with about half a dozen words to say, well I thought I could at least remember that much. So we began rehearsals. The first play was about a prisoner facing the death penalty but some late evidence had come to light that might have got him off. Four main parts were the Prison Governor, Minister, Prisoner, the prisoner's girl friend and the prison warden. The producer was also the prison governor but as it was difficult for him to act as well as produce he asked me, having little to do, to read his lines so be could concentrate on directing the play. I apparently did so well I was asked to take the part. At the next rehearsal I tried to remember the lines. The first line I could remember, the second line I could remember but the third line my mind went a complete blank so I picked the script and continued using it. I remember afterwards going to the pub with the rest of the cast sitting there shaking, thinking I had bitten off more than I could chew and a lady member thrusting a cigarette into my hand to calm my nerves. The rehearsals continued twice a week, it was a difficult play rather heavy material and getting into the spirit of the theme was not easy and sometimes we failed. Apparently I showed no nerves during rehearsals and some would ask why? I could not answer them but I can say this that on the first night when we went on stage with our make up on and I could hear the audience chatting away on the other side of the curtain I was nervous then. Oh if something would happen so we could not put it on but it was too late the curtain was soon to open. I was first to speak when the play started and smoking the stub of a cigar I would turn to the prison padre who was looking out of the window and say, 'Has it started to rain'? He would make a reply and I would stub out the cigar in the ashtray and so it began. All went well, I needed no prompting and the play was well received. That was my debut at acting but there is more to tell. Harry fell very ill and ended up in hospital one week before the plays were to be performed. In the third play he had a part as a sheriff supervising the proceedings in a provincial court room, a Scots comedy with plenty of fun and banter. I received a letter saying as the producer had fallen ill I was being asked to take his part, the show must go on. We had an assistant producer for the first play so that took care of that and so I had another part to play. I was still learning the lines the night the play went on, but you can get away with things in a comedy that is not possible in a serious play. I enjoyed the experience and by this time I was hooked on acting. We did another play I think it was called 'Lang may yer lum reek' anyway it was a comedy about a family living in a tenement flat with lots of chimneys on top and when the sweep was called he put the brush down the neighbours lum in error. The fun was fast and furious.

I had a chance meeting with a professional actor once and I asked him about prospects in the business. He advised me against it saying there were 8 out of 10 actors out of work you never knew where your next job was coming from or if you would get one at all, but then again I might be an overnight success and never need look for work again. He gave me a ticket to attend the rehearsals of a television play in Glasgow's Theatre Royal. I spent the evening by myself in a glass balcony structure watching two men acting out a part inside a motor vehicle. On another occasion I attended an actors' conference in the Lyceum Theatre in Edinburgh. The debate I think was on free expression and several actors were complaining about the constraints on language in the theatre and the limited vocabulary they were allowed on stage. One man was saying he was prevented from using a four-letter word (quite obscene I might add) in a play presented to school children, by the headmaster. Why should there be such restraints on free speech. Well I was appalled to say the least and the whole tone of the debate was one of degradation. So I thought if I join this lot I will be more corrupt than I am now, have less work than I have now and the dole might be my only source of income for periods of time so I walked away from it and did not look back. I suppose I spent the best part of 10 years in the Y.M. but several of the buildings in the city have now closed.

When I completed my studies at the Heriot Watt College in 1957 I was given a job at the Rolls Royce, Hillington Factory in Glasgow as a Technical Engineer, as mentioned earlier and then on to Brown Bros., marine engineering firm in Edinburgh. During my time there I saw the whole office building burn down. I happened to be in the vicinity on the Saturday afternoon and saw the building ablaze from end to end. Some of the staff did not know about it until they reported for work on the Monday morning. All the drawings were saved from burning by being in fireproof drawers, but not safe from water penetration and so some were saturated to being just wet round the edges. We spent the first two weeks hanging drawings up like clothes on the line to dry them out. We then moved into an old soap factory for the next two years until the office accommodation was rebuilt. The factory office building was next door to a cemetery and many office workers view was of this grave outlook. The only excitement out of the window was the occasional funeral service; opinion on the shop floor was that when 'Browns' were finished with you they simply threw you over the wall. There was of course the retiral presentation when office workers were allowed to leave five minutes before lunch break to attend such an event if they wished. On one occasion the managing director pronounced the usual accolade on the man having spent lifetime in the business and when it came to the elderly man's time to reply he stood there in his brown overalls, well worn jacket, cap on one side of his head and said, "Well its very nice standing here in front of my fellow workers. I've been 40 years in this business and I am damn glad to be getting out of it". That was all he said and then we left to have our lunch

There was office retirals too and when I would witness one I would say to myself "is that going to be me in 25 years time?" I am now pushing forty and some would say life begins at forty, well, I can say for me life changed at forty. I felt very much confined in the office. I am really an outdoor person so I requested an interview with one of the directors. I asked him if I could be given an outdoor job and he replied in one word, "No". I sent in my notice to leave and was given back the money I had paid into superannuation so I had enough to live on for a while. Just to be able to walk up the street and feel the sun on my back that was reward in itself. I had no idea what I wanted to do, but after a period of reflection I thought I would look for a job in selling and ended up with a Double Glazing Company selling secondary windows which were fitted behind existing frames. Double Glazing was all the rage at the time, the saving on fuel bills, eliminating draughts etc had a wide appeal, many articles appeared in newspapers and magazines promoting the benefits, I could get excited about it myself, enthusiasm is an important characteristic in selling. The work involved canvassing for appointments in the mornings and going back on presentations in the evenings. I found it difficult in the beginning but regular sales training improved my performance and I began to make money and earn a good living.

Selling is an interesting profession and an honourable one, training is necessary but you learn more by experience. You were expected to convert 1 in 3 of the presentations made, but you might start off converting 1 in 6 and then gauge your performance by improving on that. Sales training was held every Monday along with the business meeting, but extra training sessions could be put on during the week. Sometimes the sales manager would go with a trainee on a presentation. One trainee was of a particularly nervous disposition and on measuring the windows he would walk all over the furniture, sofa or settee much to the consternation of his manager and house owner. The sales manager always had a few replies to newspaper adverts to hand out at the sales meetings. We were always eager to get one of these because such a lead would almost certainly result in an order. When people are being asked to part with their well earned cash they need assurance and if you lack confidence then they are unable to come to a decision. You have almost to take the attitude, I don't care if you buy or not, a sense of humour helps and, of course, to sell yourself is as important as selling the product. Customers very seldom say 'Yes I will buy' or 'I'm ready to go ahead', but experienced salesmen can detect 'buying signals' which indicates that in their mind they are ready to buy. Neil Connery, brother of the film star Sean, was one of our team and I remember doing a presentation with him one night and it became obvious the man of the house was not going to give us a decision; (we were trained always to get a decision on our first call); I then told them who Neil was, hoping this would move him, the wife was impressed but the husband was not, he still would not budge and we left without the order. I was asked to chaperone a salesman on one occasion who had been off work, the reason why I was not told. He looked a pleasant chap, always a ready smile on his face. I left him on Friday night and was shocked to be told on the Monday he had hanged himself. Apparently he had made several attempts on his life, it was the usual case of mounting debts and the wife having left him, I of course was told nothing of this and I imagine he was put with me to see if my good nature would rub off on him, but to no avail.

Swiss Jaunt

In the summer of 1963 my friend and I travelled to Switzerland in a Morris Mini car leaving at 11pm on a Friday night after working all day. It was an experience I will never repeat.

Sleep was the problem while driving and it was only with extreme effort I was able to stave off the inevitable. At one time I got down on the back seat for my two hours off and it seemed I was awakened immediately to take the wheel again. However, arriving in London in the early hours of the morning we were awake for our journey south.

On arrival in Calais the rain was lashing down and this persisted all the way to Belgium the long French roads appearing very drab with cyclists looking like drowned rats, the dreary scene only enlivened by passing famous place names like Dunkirk.

In Ostende we obtained accommodation for the night and a more than welcome meal. In the morning, however, I was still looking forward to my bacon and egg breakfast but what a disappointment to see only bread, butter and jam on the table my introduction to the continental breakfast.

On our way to Brussels the road was made up of cement panels and we had to put up with a regular boom boom in our ears for miles along the way. On stopping for petrol while leaving the city we noticed water running out of the engine. The diagnosis from the mechanic was a broken water pump which necessitated an over night stay in the city. I will always remember Brussels for that wonderful building the Palais of Justice but not, however for the cleanliness of the streets.

We were making for the summer house on Lake Constance of a family my friend had stayed with the year before. Through Belguim, Luxembourg. France, Germany and then Switzerland in the evening, but on arrival at our destination the house was empty so we looked for alternative accommodation. Calling at the nearest hotel they only had a single room available with a single bed We pondered, it had been a long drive and now getting dark we were not prepared to look further and so took what was on offer; it proved to be a bad decision.

The hotel was next to a main line station and trains trundled through all night I don't think I got a wink of sleep. The sequence of events was first; a bell would ring warning motorists that the level crossing gates were about to close, followed by squeaks from the crying out for oil hinges and then a clatter as the gates came together. There would-then be a poignant silence followed by a distant rumble which got loud-er and louder as the train approached and then all hell was let loose, like the sound of a thousand galloping horses as the train passed through the station the sound receding as it went by and the squeak and clatter of the gates returning to their original position. If the train stopped there was the usual noise of carriage doors opening and banging shut accom-panied by shouts from porters. The two of us in a single bed, unable to close the window because of the extreme heat. This went on the whole night. Silence followed each passing train until the next monster was due and the whole performance was repeated. It did not make Switzerland an attractive place on my first visit to the country.

Returning to Lake Constance to meet up with our frlends there we then moved on to Basel and then drove south to Lucerne. One of the most characteristic features of town is an old roofed wooden bridge crossing the river Reuss, which flows into the lake, called Kapellbrucke. It was built in 1333, partly demolished in 1834-54 and recently suffered a fire but has since been rebuilt. Lake Lucerne was beautiful and gave us sight of the mountains beyond which was our next destination. Up, up, we travelled to Andermat high in the Swiss Alps and arranged accommodation there in a hotel where we were given the bridal suite, just right for two eligible bachelors.

Switzerland is the most mountainous country in Europe and for me the most attractive part of the region. The mass of grey rock topped with white snow and floored wlth lush green grass, the three colours dominate the scene. The following day we had to travel higher, to 9000ft, where we reached the Furkapass. At this elevation the snow lay all around, the air was crisp and clear. The Pass, actually a fork between two peaks,was opened to wheeled traffic in 1867 and is one of the high-est road passes in Europe. It commands grand views of the country round about including the Rhone Glacier which we would eventually reach. Our next visit was to the Sustenpass at a lower elevation but more attractive and a small lake with icebergs called the lake of death;

if anyone falls in they will not come out alive, it's that cold. Then on to the Rhone Glacier where it is possible to walk through a tunnel cut into the ice itself. A nice way to cool off if it is hot. These mountain roads are only open five months of the year so it is a very busy tourist season

At a much lower altitude we reached Interlaken, so-called because of its position between the lakes of Thun and Brienz. It was very expensive in town so we drove on to a village a few miles distant, and at the Station Hotel we got accommodation at half the price they were charging in town. After settling in we drove back to a restaurant where we enjoyed a traditional Swiss dish called Fondue. It was daylight when we arrived in town, and dark when we left, and neither of us could remember the way back to the hotel. After several attempts then having to turn back into town,each blaming the other for our lack of observation, we finally had to stop and admit we were lost. Fumbling to see if we could find maps,one of us looked to the left and through the window,a familiar sign, could it be, yes it was, quite by accident, or with help from God, we had stopped outside our shelter for the night.

The sun was shining the following morning and through our bedroom window we could see the triple mountains of the Eiger, Jungfrau and Monch. The dazzling white of the snow covered peaks gave us a wonderful send off for our next port of call which was the capital, Bern. We made our way to the government buildings to learn something of the country's administration. The country is made up of cantons, now 26 in all begun by the union of three cantons in 1291. The country will always remain neutral, it is a political philosophy we were told. At that time the women did not have the vote, that was to be permanent too according to the courier, "We do not ape other countries," he told us, but since then the women have been given the vote. Three languages are spoken in parliament, German, French and Italian and translation made for the others like they do in the United Nations. The country is approximately half Roman Catholic and half Protestant although one town may be Catholic the other mainly Protestant.

Our second last night in Switzerland was spent in an hotel owners house. Torrential rain and a thunder storm made us look for shelter, but the hotel, a few miles from Bern was full up and this alternative provided by the hotel owner was most welcome. Making our way back to the hotel for a meal the road was lit up by frequent flashes of lightening

My parents 25th wedding anniversary

illuminating the way ahead.

The following day arriving in Basle we took a boat trip on the Rhine where we were told during the war years German and French soldiers viewed each other across the stretch of water shouting abuse at each other in keeping with the mood of the times.

On the day of our departure my friend had an interview for possible employment in the country which meant a late start on our way home. Driving fast through France to make Ostende by the evening we had an encounter with a vehicle container which seemed to be carrying a supply of whitewash which was spuming out the back. When we tried to overtake our windscreen became opaque and we were unable to do so. Having to slow down and keep a hundred yards distant we were glad to see the vehicle take a turn to the right and give us a clear road ahead. In Ostend we parked the car in the town square to look for accommodation,but were soon told by the hotel owners to remove our car as it was market day in the morning and we would be unable to get out. Well in the morning what a transformation. I had parked the car half way up a street leading into the square,but the stalls went away up beyond that; I was just able to get out and allow a smiling stall holder to fill the vacant place.

Back in Dover we had to contend with Custom Officials. Questioned by a blue eyed, blonde hair young man it seemed like an interrogation,but we had nothing to hide. Custom Officers were very strict in those days quite unlike those on the Continent. On the other extreme,when we approached the Luxembourg border,we were travelling at speed and not able to stop,we gave the uniformed official a wave, he gave us a wave back and we were in the country. Our friends in Basle when visiting Britain were kept below deck for the entire Channel crossing,the husband complaining bitterly that he had been denied an opportunity to view the White Cliffs of Dover.

Switzerland is a beautiful country especially the Alps. The comparison is always with the Scottish Highlands,but the difference is I think, that our mountains are fun mountains, you can climb them if you feel energetic enough to do so. Whereas the huge masses of grey rock comprising the Alps can only be looked at in wonder and awe.

CHAPTER 6

Family Bereavement

I was a salesman for about three years when in 1972 my father died. Two weeks previously my mother on returning from a visit to her brother and sister fell and broke her ankle and ended up in hospital. I went to see her two days later and apart from her leg in plaster, she was fine. She asked me if I would go home and bring an article from the house to her. I left immediately, and on entering the house found my father very upset. He was sitting on the edge the sofa looking thin, his clothes seemed to be hanging from him and he could barely speak, but I could just hear him say, 'Oh Gilbert I'm glad you've come'. He had made some attempt at dinner and when my sister arrived we sat down to have a meal. In the afternoon, we went out to a golf course and watched golfers playing and had a half pint of beer in the club house, golf was his main recreation all his life. In view of the situation at home, I phoned the office to say I would not be in that day, I was now working for a window conversion company, I decided to stay at home and when I made my morning calls from the office I would take my father with me. Every day we visited the hospital and my father never had a bad day all week. It was the Sunday morning, a beautiful day, my father ate a hearty breakfast and then sat in the chair to listen to a sermon on the wireless. He remarked at one point, 'You wonder why there is trouble in Northern Ireland after a sermon like that'. It proved to be his last words. I watched him out of the window as he walked away to purchase his Sunday morning newspapers. I decided to wait until he got back before I left to go to church. I moved my car out of the garage path to be ready for the off on his return and as I moved out on to the street I saw a man lying on his back on the pavement at the end of the road. Nothing registered then, I thought to myself a workman has fallen, his brown sports outfit seemed to indicate this. As I backed my car into the kerb I could still see this man and now a small number of people were gathering around. As I stepped out of the car a lady ran up the street and said, 'It's your father'. I ran down as fast as I could, someone had already phoned for an ambulance and one soon arrived. The ambulance man shone a torch into his eye and shook his head. I went into the vehicle with my father and when he arrived at the hospital I was shown into a room and five minutes later a doctor came in and confirmed he was dead. I then came home to tell my sister and phone my brother, the next job was to tell my mother in hospital. Being a Sunday morning it was very quiet when I got there, but I did find someone and explained the situation to her and then she asked me to sit in a small room. In time my mother arrived on crutches smiling, but when told of the sad news she completely broke down. In view of the situation, the doctor allowed her to go home. It was a quick call by any standard. The funeral was on Wednesday, most people in attendance were Shetlanders and some close friends came to the house. It proved to be a social occasion not quite appropriate for a funeral but then if dad had been there he would have wanted that way there was nothing he liked better than having friends to the house.

My mother and sister wanted me to stay with them now that there was no man in the house so I got my own house ready to let out to students. Selling means long hours at work and with the sudden bereavement at home I was beginning to feel under some stress. I went to the doctor and he sent me to the hospital for a check up, and when reporting to him the following Monday he said take a week off and come back and see me next week, next Monday it was the same, and the next, and the next, it went on for nine weeks. Speaking to a colleague salesman he asked me what was wrong, I could not tell him, so I got out the doctors line which I could not read myself but he was able to decipher 'Nervous Exhaustion'. Well I knew it was exhaustion but not the type you can cure with a night sleep. I gave up my job with the Window Conversion Firm and kept myself busy getting the house ready for the students but some days I would suffer from terrible depression so much so I simply wanted to die myself. This way I was not much help to my mother and sister who were also deeply saddened by the sudden bereavement. One day it got so bad I simply had to talk to someone. I had now moved to a surgery near where I was staying, it was a beautiful summer evening, no one wanted to see the doctor on such a fine night I had the place to myself. He was a young doctor and adopted a rather sleepy attitude always trying to stifle a yawn. I talked to him and talked, and talked, and talked, he never tried to stop me, I talked on while he lay back slouching in his chair. I can't remember now what I said but when he was quite sure I had finished he said slowly, 'Gilbert I'm going to put you on a course of pills, you must promise me to take them, you must promise'. They were valium pills I had to take three a day and two before I went to bed at night. I went around in a daze half asleep all day taking the two pills before I retired at night, my knees nearly buckled as I climbed into bed. I reported back to the doctor in one week's time and he told me to continue with the treatment and after three weeks I was able to let up on the pills only taking one when I felt I needed one. It proved to be the turning point.

There were no obvious signs that my father was ill. My mother was surprised when he came home early from playing golf having taken a funny turn on the course, once he took a turn in the Bank and was shown into the manager's office to recuperate. When I let the doctor out of the house after a visit he turned to me and said, 'I think your father has had a chill'. He died a few days later.

After one year in selling I was able to purchase my first house and with £600.0p in the Bank acquired property in Dalkeith Road. It was a ground flat with a bay window at the front and its own front door, two large rooms, two small rooms, a large hallway and bathroom. The price was £2800.0p and I had to put down 10% or £280.0p deposit. I discovered after purchase that there was a damp problem, rising damp was always present in older property. I obtained a 50% grant from the Council towards the cost of removing the plaster from the walls inside

3 or 4 feet from the floor, replastering with waterproof material clearing the under floor ventilation which had been blocked by raising the front path too high and installing storage central heating. After decoration I could say the house was quite comfortable.

CHAPTER 7

The Camera and I

Well I had enough of working for a master, could I now do my own thing. While a member of the Rosebank Camera Club in my draughts-man days, I won first prize two years running for best picture. The first year it was judged by popular vote, the next year by a member of the Edinburgh Camera Club. With the experience of selling behind me I thought I would try running my own photographic business. I spent £40.00 on developing equipment, I already had a camera, turned an attic room in my parent's house into a dark room and that gave me a start. I began with social photography working in hotels and social clubs and through contacts there I got the occasional wedding to do. I started off doing black and white prints but soon turned to colour. The business was building up and so I started looking for premises and was lucky to find property in Easter Road on my first call to an estate agent's office. His office was available to let and so we agreed on a rent of a £1000.00 down and payment of £11.00, per week. The property had been fully modernised and consisted of a front shop, two large rooms at the back, a box room, bathroom, and a large walk-in cupboard which I used as a dark room, and so when the estate agent's moved out I moved in. When the students left my house in Dalkeith Road after their studies were over I put the house on the market and sold it for £6175.0p, this price increase in just over three years. When the lawyer had taken his fee and paid off the mortgage, I had been paying a little over £20.00. per month, he sent me a cheque for over £3600.0p . I never had so much money in my life this helped me of course to set up the business. The property was ideal in every way and so at a later stage I contacted the owner regarding the possibility of buying, he was agreeable and I think we settled on a price of £4000.00 however when I spoke to a surveyor friend of mine he advised against buying. The building is known to every surveyor in the city as lying in a fault that runs from the city to shore and broken lintels, cracked walls are evidence of that. I could of course have continued with the rent but I was not too happy living and working in such a place with the possibility of things getting worse and perhaps having to move out at a moment's notice. I borrowed £2550.00 from the Bank to buy a jeweller's shop on the main London Road near Abbeyhill as the owner was retiring. I sold a small shop which I purchased round the corner from Easter Road for £1500.0p so I was now £1000.0p in overdraft to the Bank. At the same time I purchased a flat in Milton Street for £3600.0p putting a £1000.0p down and taking out a mortgage for the balance. The year was 1975/76.

I did every kind of photography, weddings, social, portraits, passports, copy work, commercial and legal. A man came into the shop one day and asked if I would come to the house and take pictures of his friend who had been the subject of assault and rape. I did not know what to expect when I got there but after a few introductory remarks the man said to the woman, 'now you know what to do', the lady replied 'Yes I know what to do' whereupon she dropped her skirt, she had nothing on underneath and then I was asked to take photographs. Commercial work consisted of buildings and objects to photograph. I worked for the Scottish Development Agency and they would send me all over the place in the east of the country. One assignment was to the Methil Oil Rig yard in Fife and I had to photograph an Oil Rig Jacket which was shortly to be launched. Some of the cranes on caterpillar wheels were enormous the wheels themselves being the height of a man. I noticed that bulldozers were moving a cement mixture about on which these giant cranes would move. I had to have an escort with me in case I wandered somewhere that might be dangerous. We were both wearing helmets and I got somewhere ahead of my companion and walked into this cement mixture thinking it would bear my weight and I fell in up to my knees. I put my hand out to steady myself and damaged the camera I was holding, the escort then ran up and pulled me out of the bath. Every week-end I would be taking wedding photographs, however I have left the subject of Wedding Photographer to another chapter.

Another commercial job was to photograph the opening of a Granada Television shop in a new arcade in Edinburgh. The opening was to be performed by William Roach of 'Coronation Street' fame and his wife. They were both very pleasant as they talked with customers and signed autographs. About one year later the same actor was asked to open another Granada shop in a different part of the city. I arrived in this new arcade with the usual number of shoppers about, no one in the front shop, I wandered into the back premises and someone grabbed my hand and shook it warmly, it was him, William Roach, he recognised me from the previous occasion, surely a reversal of roles while I was trying to find the celebrity, it was the celebrity who found me.

Wedding Photographer

Having photographed a fair number of weddings, this much I can say there are no two alike. Wasps were a problem on one occasion and trying to get the bridesmaids to pose was next to impossible. The bride told me when she collected the photographs she heard a wasp buzzing about under her dress during the ceremony. It was just as well one did not get under the ministers cloak or that would have made the wedding most unusual. On another occasion I was standing in front of the communion table waiting to take a picture of the signing when I saw the priest looking in my direction and talking, but I could not hear what he was saying 'I hope he is not complaining about me being in too prominent a position' I thought, when one of the party came up to me and said 'The Father wants to know if you can lend him a pen for the signing'. On this occasion I was happy to oblige. I was standing at the church door waiting on the wedding party to arrive and when the bridesmaids car arrived the mother's first words to me were 'You are not our photographer'. I checked with the minister that the names I had were the names he had, they were. I then returned to the church door only to find the mother and bridesmaids climbing back into the car, they had arrived at the wrong church. The middle aged bride whose garter fell down while I was about to take the photograph. I tried to indicate to the groom the problem, he eventually got the message and said turning to his bride, 'Darling your garter has come down'. She quickly removed it and held it in her hand while the photograph was taken. One Catholic wedding nearly resulted in a nasty accident for myself. The interior of the chapel had many statutes all recognised by the priest who on passing each one bent the knee in reverence. I had been told earlier by the caretaker where I should stand behind a pillar to take pictures during the ceremony however when the priest saw me as the official photographer he insisted on showing me himself. He entered the building and I was hurrying to catch up with him and on turning sharp right to enter the chapel I nearly fell over the spiritual head of the congregation down on one knee, head deeply bowed in reverence to the alter. Only by taking quick evasive action was I able to avoid what could have been a nasty accident for myself and camera. On two occasions I have had to act as best man as well as photographer. The first time was an Irish couple married in a registrar's office. An elderly lady out doing her shopping was prevailed upon by the registrar to act as bridesmaid so in she came with her shopping basket and coat buttoned up to the neck. The bride was not wearing her wedding dress because she thought that would make her too conspicuous. She had booked a room in a nearby hotel where she would put on her wedding dress for the photographs. The couple went to Spain for their honeymoon and I had to have the photographs ready on their return a week later. Calling at my home on a Saturday night the bride explained there is no such thing as a registrar office wedding in Ireland, all weddings take place in church hence, no photographs at the office. She had visited Edinburgh as a child and thought it a beautiful place and if she ever got married she would get married there. She also said she was happy to be going home as she vas given a puppy dog shortly before she left and all the time she was in Spain she was concerned the dog might be pining for her. The second time was an American couple who came over to Scotland, he a doctor, she a nurse. I was only asked on arriving at the church if I would be best man. I had been to this church often and the minister's address is

74

always the same, at one point in the ceremony he asks the congregation 'Is there anyone here who knows just cause why this couple should not be legally married' there is a short pause, nobody speaks and so he continues. I did not think it necessary to say this with such a small gathering of four but he did. Having only met the couple the day before I did not feel qualified to give an answer one way or the other. Later when the photographs were taken I had to get the minister to take some shots while I put my other hat on as best man. Following this we all retired to the manse for tea,

I don't take tea so when the minister was about to pour mine I had to refuse. the conversation went. something like this:

Minister "Tea?"
Reply "No thanks, I don't take tea".
M "You don't take tea?"
R "No"
M "You don't take tea?"
R "No"
M "You never take tea?"
R "No, I'll have a glass of milk"
M "You want a glass of milk. You don't take tea?"
R "No"
M "You never take tea?"
R "I never take tea"
M "You never take tea?"
R "I'll have a glass of milk"

Whereupon he retired to the kitchen and returned holding high a glass of milk saying. "Is this what you want?" "Thank you very much" I said and he laid it on the table. Weddings where horse drawn carriages are used add to the picture quality although one time it must have been unpleasant for the couple because of the odour coming off the horse. I have a picture of a couple in an 1928 Austin in showroom condition as if it had been bought the day before. Videos have become popular now and I have seen myself several times on telly directing groups for still pictures. Only once have I experienced a bride upset and crying during the ceremony. She had an identical twin sister who was unmarried. She first appeared at the end of an L shaped path which led up to the church door carrying her dress and train in front of her like she was pushing a barrow, a rather unattractive pose for a bride. The minister was not there to greet her at the door and later said he wished he had,having not met such a nervous bride. I did the best I could with the pictures which was not helped by red blotches on her neck and body caused by her condition. At the reception she was quite worn out and hapless but her handsome groom remained calm and smiling through it all. I learned later she completely broke down at 12 noon for her wedding at 3 o'clock. I am not a drinking man but have often been enticed by some well meaning slightly intoxicated individual to the bar for a refreshment but have had to refuse, however on one occasion it was next to impossible to do so. I got involved with a small circle of friends including the bride and groom who were emigrating to America to begin a new life there. A glass of champagne was put down in front of each one whether they wanted it or not. A toast was then given for the couples future and we all drank our champagne. I had never tasted the stuff before and never will again; a taste somewhere between rubber and straw, those who can drink it without pulling a face, I raise my hat to them.

One of the more bazaar occasions happened early on in my career when I used to take photographs for another firm who had anything from 12 to 15 weddings to do each Saturday and so needed extra help. However this Saturday I was doing one of my own and arrived first at the hotel,where the ceremony and reception both were taking place, just in front of the minister who went straight up to reception and asked the way to the bar. When the wedding party arrived the mother came up to me and said had the minister arrived I said 'yes' and showed her where he was sitting.The ceremony took place in a room,I did not enter until they were ready for the signing. This done we all tripped out to the front garden to take photographs in the sunshine. I found things difficult as I had never met the bride and groom before having dealt only with the mother and that is not always a good thing, they looked on me as if someone had gate crash the party. I could not get them to pose properly and to cut a long story short the photographs did not come out very well. The following Saturday I was doing a wedding for the other firm when I was surprised to see the couple there who had been married the week before and more surprised when I saw the mother who came up to me and said 'I don't want you to take the photographs'. Now the mother had a member of the family married one week and another member of the family married the following week and here was the same lousy photographer having made a mess of the first wedding about to do the same with the second. If ever there was a time when the ground would open up and swallow me this was it. It proved to be a very different wedding with the bride in white array and the groom in Highland outfit with cravat, they could pose so well my task was made easy I only had to press the button. Of course I did not see the second set of photographs but the manager said they were satisfactory and was able to show me one with the couple in splendid pose on the hotel balcony. However it was a situation I did not want to repeat and concentrated on my own work from then on. One register office I attended the registrar would put the couple at ease by telling the same story "Well it is a nice day today not like the day when I got married it rained from morning to night. Still I can say that from that day on there has been sunshine in my life, at least so the wife keeps telling me." I am reminded of the time I was best man at my friend's wedding. We got there early and were shown into the vestry by the minister. As we sat there we noticed a pile of neatly folded white handkerchiefs on his desk and as he put on the garb he put one handkerchief at the back of his neck, one under his armpit and one under the other and then he was aware of us watching him "You will be wondering why I am doing this" he said. "Well", he continued "I was taking a wedding once and the couple were so nervous they conveyed their nervousness to me I began to sweat and thought I was going to pass out, ever since I have taken this precaution". After he got rid of three handkerchiefs it is left to the imagination of the reader where the others went.

It seems a pity but a hard fact that many of weddings I have attended will end in separation,the divorce rate today being high. May I be allowed to make a small contribution to this problem. I feel that confusion is brought about by the writers of romantic novels giving one aspect of living together and the church with its interpretation of the husband and wife relationship. The words spoken at a wedding ceremony are of a commanding love or as one minister put it a sacrificial love whereas the novel writers talk about an emotional love. More emphasis should be placed on the words spoken at a wedding ceremony and less emphasis on the 'Falling in Love' principle. "Will you love this man, Will you love this woman" that is the commitment made one to the other in a public place, in front of witnesses, relations and friends. That is the vows made to each other and is sealed by contract. When problems come along that can be the testing time and too many couples are not making the necessary effort to overcome their problems and seek,to them,the only way out and that is divorce. It is a moral problem, a lack of commitment and a lack of understanding of the marriage partnership. It is a complex area, I am no marriage counsellor but leave you with this thought as my contribution to an ever increasing problem.

FAMILY

A little bird sat on a cherry-tree limb,
And a dear little maiden listened to him;
For each word of his song, though loud and clear,
Was meant for nobody else's ear.
"Sweet! sweet!" he said, "You'll surely agree—
The man the head of the house should be."

"That's all very well for a bird, you know,"
The maiden answered in whispers low;
"But a woman, I think, has a right to reign
As a sovereign queen of her own domain!"
"Sweet! sweet!" sang the little bird saucily,
"The man the head of the house should be."

"But what if it happens," the maiden said,
"That the very one I may choose to wed,
Though worthy of love, is too weak to rule
For even a man may be a fool!"
"Sweet! sweet!" said the bird, ere she made her plea,
"The man the head of the house should be."

Away flew the bird to its cozy nest;
Deep, deep went his song to the maiden's breast.

And she found it true as the bird had sung,
In the summertime when the maid was young;
"The man the head of the house should be!
But the wife—the heart of the house is she!"

Anonymous

CHAPTER 8

No Parking Ticket

When I moved to the south side of Edinburgh I used to park my car in a square off the main thoroughfare while I did some shopping. On this occasion on returning to my car I saw two lady traffic wardens standing by and a yellow form wrapped around the windscreen wiper blade. "What's this"? I said. They replied that this area was now a residential parking zone and in consequence I had incurred a fine of £2.00. I had parked here often and no one had informed me of the new regulation but the wardens were quick to point to a sign indicating the change. I paid the fine within one week and received a receipt by return. Some weeks later I received a letter from the police saying I had parked my car in this square and had not paid the fine. I wrote back saying I had paid the fine, there must be some mistake and gave them the number of the receipt. A week or two passed when two policeman came into my shop premises. "Are you Mr Williamson" also giving my two Christian names, "I am". "You parked your car in St. Patrick's Square and have not paid the fine." I told them I had paid the fine and was able to produce the receipt as proof. The policeman examined the form then replied, "this shows that you have paid £2.00. sir, but it does not say what you have paid £2.00. for." I was beginning to get a little irritated.

"Now look here", I said, "I have committed an offence, I have paid the fine, I have shown you the receipt and now you say it's not worth the paper it's written on, what more can I do?" We chatted some more and before the policeman left he read out the charge again. On this day in April I had parked my car in a residential parking zone, etc, etc. I looked at the date on the receipt and it said August. "Did you say April?" I asked the policeman, he confirmed it was April, I know of no offence in April. He then suggested that I go to the payments office in the High Street and obtain details from them, meanwhile he would have to press the charge. I went to the High Street at lunch time and the lady could confirm there was an offence in August, the fine had been paid, there was also an offence in April the fine had not been paid. I asked for more details and she was able to give the address in the same square where I was supposed to have parked. I thanked her and went back to the square and to the address to see if it would jog my memory, it did not, no entry either in my diary. I was left puzzled and went home. Later I received a letter from the authorities, did I plead guilty or not guilty to the offence. By this time I was a little annoyed and wrote back pleading not guilty. In time I received a letter fixing my trial for August next year, it was now November of the previous year. I could not believe it, so far ahead, I could forget it in that time, maybe they want me to forget it. One day while out walking I met one of the police who came into the shop. I told him I had received a letter from the court and had pleaded not guilty to the charge. "Good" he said "What date is the trial" "Next August " I said "August" he stammered. "I could forget it by then" I replied. "That's what to do, just forget about it, in fact go on holiday and enjoy yourself". Such was the advice from the law.

Well the months rolled on, away at the back of my mind was the trial date August, the day came and passed and at the end of the month two policeman came into the shop. One was the same fellow that offered the above advice. "Mr Williamson", "Yes", "Bad news for you I'm afraid, you did not show up for your trial". I was about to say yes and you told me not to but I remained silent. "What trial" as if I did not know. "The parking offence, you are in contempt of court, will you accompany us to the station, you are under arrest." My jaw dropped to the floor, "Now look here", I said, "you come in off the street telling me I have to accompany you to the police station, I've got work to do, I am busy, it is not possible to come right now, quite impossible, try some other time". "Well could you come tomorrow morning"?, the policeman said sheepishly. The next morning a van arrived at 8.00 am. I was placed on the seat between the two policeman one driving, we got out at the police station and walked to the reception desk. I had to empty my pockets of all contents but left with a handkerchief. "We don't like to do this but someone might jump on you in the cell", the policeman said. My heart sank a little. They allowed me to keep a book to read I brought along to pass the time. I was led along a corridor then a right turn to the first door on the left. On opening and looking inside my mind was filled with horror. Five or more old men lying on the floor, some I recognised as the city down-and-outs, cups of tea on the floor, half eaten rolls there too and the cell looked old and dirty. My first impulse was to run for it, but my way was barred by police officers. In I went and heard the door slam behind me. The feeling of despair and agony of soul was hard to describe, what am I doing here, some younger men were lying behind the door, "What are you doing here" I was asked. "Parking fine", I replied. "They put you in here for a parking fine?" It wasn't really true I was in for contempt of court. I was offered tea, then water, I put some to my lips, I sat down it was hot, the floor was black and uneven, I sat on one of the benches, I noticed an open toilet in one corner of the cell. I buried my head in the book and tried to shut out all that was around me. One old man kept groaning and moaning, but little was said . One man sat on the toilet seat his trousers round his ankles. How long will I be here? How long will I be here? About an hour or so passed then the cell door opened and an officer breezed into the cell. "Everybody out" he said. I sat there transfixed almost glued to the seat while they all moved out. He looked at me and said "you too". I went with him up a flight of stairs and was shown into another cell. This one was much smaller and I had the company of the old man who was still moaning. There was nowhere to sit down unless on the toilet seat. About ten minutes passed, I could hear the bells on the clock tower outside then a young blonde foreign man was shown in. He had a piece of paper in his hand, walked up and down the cell looking very agitated. I asked him could I help. He showed me the piece of paper and in very broken English explained he had been in a jeweller's shop and picked up a ring. With his girl friend they walked to the window to have a better look at it in the light and was pounced on by the store detective. Now he was in the cell facing a charge of attempted theft. About 25 minutes passed and I was taken out of the cell to meet a lawyer. To my surprise and his we knew each other, we had been in the Scouts together, I was his Scoutmaster. "What are you doing here sir", he said. I explained the whole matter to him and he replied, 'You do not need my help, just speak to the judge in the way you have spoken to me and you will be all right". An officer shouted "This way quickly". I was then shown into my third cell of the morning. This cell was larger with a partition down the middle so that you could not see who was sitting opposite. There were only about three or four of us there including a man with a strong Irish accent who on showing me a piece of paper asked me to read what was on it. "Arrested for drunk and disorderly fine £1.00." I read out. He thanked me most kindly and said he had been arrested on the same charge one year ago and the fine was £1.00. then and when you think of inflation in that time etc.

It turned out that this cell was directly behind the court because when I was called out and made a left turn I found myself among a lot of people. I dare not look at any of them and fortunately I had to turn my back on them to face the Judge. I gave my explanation as best I could, for my non-appearance at court. The judge smiled and said he accepted my explanation and said that I would be glad to know a second court was now being built which should cut down the waiting time to about half, did I plead guilty or not guilty. 'Not guilty", I replied whereupon two ladies sitting below the judge starting fumbling about with papers on the desk. I was led out of the chamber and asked to pay a £10.00. bail. Then I had the articles returned to my pockets I moved outside a free man again.

Now the whole purpose of going through this charade was to find out why I had received no notification of the offence. After all you cannot pay a fine when you have received no notification of an offence in the first place. At various times throughout the process I was asked if I pleaded guilty or not guilty. Presumably if I had said guilty I could have brought the proceedings to an end, but I had to find out.

Three weeks later I appeared in the brand new court room. Five witnesses were arrayed against me, two policeman, two traffic wardens and a clerk, I had no witnesses. When the judge asked one of the policeman who was the man you saw in the shop an accusing arm and finger was pointed in my direction, (my black uniformed friend who told me to forget about the trial). Then the lady warden was asked where did she place the form, she replied on the windscreen. When asked what sort of day it was she replied "it was wet". I was then allowed to ask a question. "Would it have been possible for me to have driven off and not see the form on the windscreen". She replied in the negative. It was then obvious what had happened, it had never adhered to the glass and had simply dropped off.

I was asked to pay three pounds, one pound more than the original fine. The various court officials seemed to adopt an attitude I was wasting their time, there was much more serious matters for the court to consider. Maybe the reader will think the same. But some fault surely must lie with the law by not making sure I received notification of the offence. Speaking to a traffic warden friend he said "I always wrap the yellow form round the windscreen wiper blade" which I believe is the common practice now.

CHAPTER 9

Spiritual Matters

I would like to stop my personal and family history here to concentrate on activities and interests which I have pursued during my life, the first one is religion.

I was brought up in the Church of Scotland Presbyterian Faith and remained a member until the year 1976. I changed my digs four times from 1962 when I left home to 1970 when I purchased my first house. Settled in my new home I looked for a church to join and took my lines along to St. Cuthbert's at the West End of Edinburgh, a city church. I loved listening to the organ there and they had a beautiful choir, so approaching the associate minister after the evening service I handed him my lines, he shook hands welcomed me as a new member but was somewhat taken aback when he saw I was an elder. I fully expected to be called to the session but no invitation was extended. I continued to attend church usually at the evening service. Coffee and eats were provided following the service and I usually went there and got to know one or two members. But that was the only involvement over a period of years. Now during my years as a salesman I had very little social life and I was making money but the continual nose to the grindstone so to speak was wearing me out. Following my father's death I was asked to join the Edinburgh and District Shetland Association, my father had been a Trustee of the Association for many years. At the first A.G.M. I attended I was voted on to the council and one year later was appointed Junior Vice Chairman. In 1973 a general election was called by the then Prime Minister, Edward Heath, during a miners strike, I remember, and it seemed to me to be an irresponsible decision to plunge the country into an election before the strike was settled. I am neither a Conservative or Labour supporter as I consider these class parties, you join one or the other depending on your position in life. A working man votes Labour etc so I helped out the Scottish National Party during the election campaign. I also believe in a parliament for Scotland and feel the country would be better served by people living and working in the country rather than what amounts to remote government from London. The only Assembly we have here is of course the General Assembly of the Church of Scotland which meets once a year and I always pay a visit when it is in session. I feel it is the only representative body of people in the country talking and discussing issues of vital importance to our national life, but its influence on peoples lives is minimal and I think that is a great pity. The membership of the national church continues to fall, we used to console ourselves by saying as the numbers become fewer the quality gets better, but we were clutching at straws it was not a happy situation especially for the young people who we were responsible for. It was a matter of concern for the older generation in that the young might be led astray and follow paths that led to erosion of principals and geology. It says in Proverbs Ch. 11 V. 14, "Where no counsel is, the people fall: but in the multitude of counsellors there is safety". It is therefore a matter of concern when the counsellors are becoming fewer. I remember one visit I paid to the Assembly I was not sure if it was in session or not so I asked the man at the door, he looked at me straight in the eye and said "You are not going in there are you" I said that was my intention yes 'Well I am surprised at you" he said "I thought you would be at the football in Glasgow today" No I said and asked him if it had begun "Yes" he replied "And when does it finish" I said "Finish" he exclaimed "It finishes whenever the last blethering skite has had his say that's when it finishes". "Have you a programme" I asked. Now on the floor there was a waste paper basket with some leaflets in it, he looked down at this and said "Is that what you want" I picked up a leaflet from the basket and entered the hall before be could make any more rude remarks. I'm sure a week of debate must get a bit tedious and yet words of wisdom and council are vitally important for the present and future generations. One minister described the Assembly as some talking sense and some talking nonsense. Well it provides a platform for all to speak their minds, put their point of view, get it off their chest and there is always a good laugh to help things along. I was continuing to build up my photographic business, I was constituency secretary for the S,N.P. in Leith and had my responsibilities in the Association so I had enough on my plate. It was then that I received a visit from the minister of St. Cuthbert's, Leonard ·Small, I had never spoken to him before and he more than surprised me by asking if I would go on the Session. Well I was unable to give him an answer. I was confused in that I expected to go on the session when I joined why was I now being asked two years further on. Time-wise I could simply not afford it. In this confused state when he phoned back a week later for my answer I declined his invitation. When I attended church the following Sunday the minister mentioned from the pulpit during his sermon that be had asked a man to become an elder, a man just starting a new business and faced with all the burdens that such a venture entails, he very nearly changed his mind about asking him, however the man had declined, how is the church to survive when such men will not undertake these responsibilities etc. etc. Well I was surprised again that he should mention this knowing that I was in the congregation. I had become an elder in the second church I joined the minister having written to me and 11 others inviting us to a meeting, 6 turned up to the meeting and 3 became elders and I was one of them. I undertook my duties as an elder but there was always a degree of uncertainty whether it was within myself or with the church I could never tell. One incident from those days remains firmly in my mind. One lady on my list to visit was very deaf, she would not open the door to anyone especially during the winter evenings but this summer night I gave her door a good knock and she let me in. She then talked about her deafness, could she get it back she found it an awful miss not being able to hear, did I think she could get her hearing back. Well I found myself in deep water and was struggling for an answer. I mumbled something that I thought she would but with not a lot of conviction in my voice, "Oh I hope so" she said "Ah find it an awful miss not being able to hear". I left her house feeling perplexed and inadequate, she was asking me for something which she knew I should be able to give and what's more I knew also that I should be able to help her in some way, but how. If I went to the minister he would probably suggest a hearing aid but that is not what she was asking for, there was something missing somewhere I felt I did not have the tools to do the job.

When the General Election was over I then read the SNP party manifesto and was surprised that I could not disagree with any part of it. The Party was known as the Tartan Tories but the papers always said the party was left of centre, however we always played down the left and right, it was the policies that were important. The constituency had its internal disputes not at all uncommon in any party as to whether we should continue with the existing candidate or bring in a new face. Such disputes are always divisive, in the end we chose neither candidate but brought in another man from a neighbouring constituency. I stood twice as a local candidate, once in a District election where I received over 500 votes and once for a Regional election where I received 901 votes, these were average figures for the SNP. at the time. I took a course on becoming a parliamentary candidate at SNP headquarters but it became clear I had gone as far as I could for the Party, I was turned down but was told I still had a contribution to make. We all express our views on political matters and have our preference for one party or the other but whether we are fit for the hurly burly of political life is another matter. I am sure Scotland will have its parliament one day but it will be a long slow process. As I write this a 129 seater assembly elected by proportional representation has been suggested for Scotland by a convention of various bodies including the Church. This is a big step forward and will I am sure form the foundation for a future Scottish Parliament.

The Shetland Association had its problems with a falling membership. Membership is limited to those coming from Shetland their spouses and offspring and if you were 5 years resident in Shetland you were also eligible to join. In the Zetland Golf Club formed in 1910 it has a similar constitution but with the words added "and their friends". If this clause had been inserted into the Associations constitution it would have helped the situation but attempts to bring about a change failed. You feel somewhat in a straight jacket when faced with a downward trend in membership and there is little you can do about it. Disagreement continued and it was not a happy situation. After I left, the Hall Premises in Pilrig Street was sold off for a considerable sum and now the Association has enough money to subsidise all the years events but are still faced with their numbers becoming fewer and fewer,

I feel that spiritual matters are very important in life and in my moving away from the Church I felt that something was missing. People were very selfish, inward-looking, contemptuous of each other and acting in an altogether unchristian manner. I was conscious of devils on one side and apathy on the other, I felt very despondent. In this mood I was ready to listen to someone, someone with a message of hope who could dispel my feeling of despair.

One night while in my flat listening to music I thought I heard a knock at the door. I really went there to see if there was anyone and was surprised to see two young girls standing side by side. One of them said, 'We are from the Church of Jesus Christ of Later Day Saints, we have a wonderful message to share with you could we come back another time and talk" or words to that affect. I was somewhat bemused and then they continued, "Could we come back on Sunday night at 6.30 pm". I said I thought that would be all right, they put an entry in their diary and with polite smiles left the scene. They had not been gone long when I suddenly realised I would not be at home at that time on Sunday. My first thought was to run after them and then I thought I'm not sure I wanted to see them anyway so I let it go. They were in my mind that Sunday night at 6.30 pm I do not like letting people down in this way. The following Wednesday there was a similar knock on the door, again I went to see if there was anyone and there were the same two girls. "Mr Williamson we called on Sunday evening you were not in would it be convenient to call now." Well I was not doing anything in particular so I invited them in. After a few introductory remarks they began the lesson and as one talked the other turned the pages of a picture book illustrating the story as it went along. Then they would change over. If that did not command your full attention they would then fire a question at you one that was usually next to impossible to answer. When they had finished, I thought too soon but they had another appointment I asked them if they would like a cup of tea they said, "No thank you". I knew little about Mormon habits then, I then asked with tongue in cheek "I suppose you want me to join the church" "No" they replied. 'No', I thought, what do they want. "Mr Williamson we would like to leave you with a Book of Mormon, we have marked a passage for you to read and we will call back again in a few day's time to pick it up", then they left with polite smiles and a handshake. For the next four months I investigated the Church. I found things very different from conventional church meetings, seeing ordinary people standing up giving their testimony, taking part in meetings, giving prayers, I was impressed. There is a Bishop but he wears no special clothing, numerous people take part in what is called the Sacrament Service talking about faith and miracles. I was impressed. Members telling me of miracles that had happened to them or their children or to someone they knew, I had never heard of this in the conventional church I was impressed. I found the Book of Mormon interesting, I could not put it down once I had started to read it, I told the missionaries this and then they would say "are you praying about the Book asking if it is true" I thought they had done well getting me to read scriptures now they wanted me to pray, I did as they said and then it became a book of spiritual truths. I read the Joseph Smith story how the angel Moroni spoke to him one night and told him where plates were hidden in a hill which he would eventually receive and from which he would translate the Book of Mormon, I knew all this was true and if anyone asks me how I know it is true I can only say as I read the words I knew it was the truth. I always wanted to be baptised by total immersion, it was the only baptism I had read about in the Bible. I remember asking my parents once when am I going to be baptised, they told me I had been baptised. I asked when. My mother said you see these babies being baptised in church don't you. I thought is that baptism? I could not believe it. Here was a chance to be baptised. Was I going to pass it up? The Book of Mormon I knew was scriptures, why had I not seen this book before and why were the other churches not using this book? Also I knew somehow that there was another Bible somewhere and this was it 'Another testament of Jesus Christ' A new Bible for these the later days. I entered the waters of baptism on 28th day of May 1976 just two days away from my birthday. So now I am a Mormon. Do I regret having made the decision now nineteen years in the church? I did not want to leave the church where I grew up and where most of my development took place to leave my friends and associates I had during those youthful years, although it must be admitted I don't see much of them now, I still go to the Assembly every year. The church faces continual financial crises, dwindling membership and when I hear of a man who murdered his mother being ordained to the ministry these are the things that make me feel unhappy so I soldier on, life still has its ups and downs, its crests and troughs "but in the multitude of counsellors there is safety", I feel safe and content in the Mormon Church.

On one occasion while the sisters were presenting a lesson there was a very loud rattle on the letter box which startled the girls. I went to the door and standing there was my Church of Scotland elder, he thrust some papers in my hand and asked me to read them and he would call back later to discuss the matter. He never ever asked to come into the house and he never made any attempt to get to know me. I returned to lay the papers aside, and after the sisters left, read what was in them. It was a request to take out a deed of covenant and pay my church contributions by standing order from the bank. After I joined the Church I wrote to the minister saying I was now baptised into the Church of Jesus Christ of Later Day Saints. I received no reply to the letter and no more calls either from the Church of Scotland elder.

As my membership of the church progressed I was raised first to Aaronic Priesthood and was told this lesser priesthood was in preparation for the Holy Priesthood called the Melchizedek Priesthood after the High Priest of that name. An explanation of this Priesthood is given in Hebrews Chapter 7, I quote below verse 2:

> Hebrews Ch. 7 V. 1 – 2. For this Melchizedeck, King of Salem, priest of the most high God, who met Abraham returning from the slaughter of the kings, and blest him; To whom also Abraham gave a tenth part of all; first being by interpretation King of righteousness and after that also King of Salem, which is, King of peace.

That rests easy with me. Holding this priesthood means that I can now:-
Name and bless children, baptise, confirm persons to the church,

administer the sacrament, administer to the sick, dedicate graves, give blessings of comfort and council etc.

In Matthew Ch. 9 at verses 20 – 22 we read :- "And, behold, a woman, which was diseased with an issue of blood twelve years, came behind him, and touched the hem of his garment: For she said within herself, if I may but touch his garment, I shall be whole. But Jesus turned him about, and when he saw her, he said, Daughter, be of good comfort; thy faith hath made thee whole. And the woman was made whole from that hour". 'Thy faith had made thee whole'. Miracles come about through faith, and faith on the part of the receiver, is as important as that of the giver. In the Priesthood we talk about the authority and the power of that priesthood. All of us raised to the priesthood have the authority but the power rests with oursclves our commitment to gospel principals and our obedience to the commandments of God. I now feel I have the tools to do the job.

CHAPTER 10

The Last Durbar

The other day I came across a family photograph of my parents and us three children. Unlike many old photographs when you are trying to date the picture (if only people would date family prints) this one was clearly identified with the date 1938 printed on the background.

It was in fact a studio photograph taken at the Glasgow Exhibition of that year. I was 10 years old at the time, my sister was nine and my younger brother three years. I tried to recall memories of that visit.

The road from Edinburgh to Glasgow was very different from today, cars too have changed a lot and the 40 odd miles between cities took much longer. I can't now remember the type of vehicle my father had at that time, but I do recall a Morris car which was very noisy and you had to shout to make yourself heard above the noise of the engine. After that my father obtained an Austin saloon which was much quieter. His first car was a model T Ford and we have photographs of him and my mother behind the wheel of this celebrated vehicle. (*See page 51.*)

Recalling the exhibition itself I can remember the vast crowds, the bright colourful buildings, the high modern outlook tower and the loud music playing in the background. The "Donkey Serenade" blaring out over the loud speaker is the tune I will always associate with this event in Ballahouston Park. The mechanical bogies that took you round the ground when you were tired of walking. The laughing mechanical clown who set others off laughing and then all the fun of the fair.

George VI opened the exhibition on 3rd. May accompanied by Queen Elizabeth. They ascended the Tower of Empire in a fast lift that moved at 500 feet a minute. The United Kingdom Pavilion had a 'Fitter Britain' exhibit and their Majesties were fascinated by a stream of ping-pong balls illustrating the circulation of the blood. Another visit was to a highland village called, An Clachan. On the flagged pavement outside a thatched cottage, Mary Morrison from Barra was spinning wool and singing an old lament 'Leaving Barra'. She told their Majesties that it was the first time she had left Barra and that she had come to the exhibition 'riding all the way in an aeroplane.'

Many events are recorded in newspaper clippings of that year 1938, most of which concentrate on the preparations for war on both sides of the English Channel. Chamberlain's well documented return from Munich waving a piece of paper and declaring 'Peace in our time' for example. Most of these things went over my head as a young boy but I do remember the launch of the largest liner in the world, the Queen Elizabeth, from the Clydebank shipyard, also the Queen Mary breaking the record for crossing the Atlantic in both directions of just under four days. Walt Disney's full length cartoon 'Snow White and the Seven Dwarfs', was showing in the cinemas and television was in its infancy. The locomotive Mallard breaking the record for steam engines of 126 miles per hour.

The purpose of the exhibition was to Instruct, Edify and to Entertain. The various Pavilions showed off their countries latest accomplishments for example the Australian Pavilion a model of the Sydney Harbour Bridge. the Scottish Engineering Pavilion scale models of ocean-going liners, and the New Zealand Pavilion a model of the longest railway tunnel within the Empire. The Irish Free State (Eire) had a large pavilion, although in many aspects it was not a member of the Empire. Northern Ireland also had a pavilion and the Lord Mayors of Dublin and Belfast toured both pavilions extremely amicably.

The spacious Concert Hall attracted famous band names such as Ambrose who had two girl vocalists, Evelyn Dall and Vera Lynn. Others were Geraldo, Henry Hall, Harry Roy and Roy Fox. Great orchestras such as the London Symphony Orchestra under the batten of Sir Henry Wood and Sir Thomas Beecham with the Philharmonic Orchestra who wrote in the visitors book, "It is a splendid hall for music, clear and not over-resonant." He also suggested it should be taken down and re-erected in some other part of the city. The American bass singer Paul Robeson filled the Concert Hall not once but twice. The morning after his second performance he visited the Clachan Village and sang two songs much to the delight and surprise of the audience. In an interview with Jack House he was asked what he thought of Scotland and the Scots and received the unlooked-for reply, "They don't read their Bible enough." It has to be said, however, in showing how times have changed,the organisers resisted all requests to have the gates open on Sunday.

Unlike previous exhibitions it was considered that an amusement park was necessary to provide "innocent merriment" for the ordinary man and his family. The formidable scenic railway was tried out by some exalted visitors such as a high ranking religious leader who pronounced after he got off, "Well, that was grand." A young Canadian by the name of Billy Butlin, who would shortly become famous as a holiday camp chief, assumed responsibility for the 16 acre site.

It was hoped that the exhibition would become permanent but the war clouds hanging over Europe put paid to that. In the post war years it became evident that the Empire was lost as the Union Jack was pulled down in country after country to be replaced by the national flag. In 1997 when Hong Kong was handed over to the Chinese it was dubbed "the end of Empire." It has been a slow lingering death and now Britain must take her place among the community of European nations

Was the event a success, the last Durbar, the last great assemblage of Empire? The answer has to be an unqualified 'yes'. The unanimous recollection 60 years on, of those who attended the great event is of the tremendous joy and delight, the overpowering sense of wonder which they derived from what was on show at that esteemed Park in Glasgow.

CHAPTER 11

Faith and Freedom

I give below a few anecdotes during the time of the war. The conflict began on the 3rd September 1939 when I was eleven years old and ended in May 1945 when I was going on seventeen. One year later I was called up for two years National Service. I remember well the day war broke out. It was a Sunday morning the family were sitting round the table for breakfast when an announcement was made over the radio that the Prime Minister would be addressing the nation at eleven o'clock that morning. A feeling of despondency filled our home so much so that my sister began to cry. My mother took her and my younger brother a walk while my father and I listened to the broadcast and the Prime Minister Neville Chamberlain say that there was now a state of war existing between our country and Germany. I remember feeling very brave sitting with my father listening to this when the others were unable to do so. Looking back I have often wondered why the announcement was made at that time in the morning when most people would be at church. We opened the shop on Sunday afternoons and this Sunday was like any other Sunday many people about chatting and laughing. A group of young people, youths,would always gather at the corner of the street to talk and laugh for a while before breaking off in couples and then going their separate ways. One difference however was when one lady who owned a shop nearby came in greatly concerned there was a man shouting in the street 'They are bombing London, they are bombing London, is it true?' It was only a rummer the first of many that would follow during the war years. The first air raid by the Germans was the following day on the Forth Bridge although I believe the first air raid of the war was carried out by our planes over Germany on the afternoon evening on the Sunday

We built the Anderson shelter in the back garden half submerged in the ground as per instructions, were issued with gas masks which we carried all the time, made blackouts for the house and shop to restrict stray light, blinds were fitted to car head lights, the iron gates in the front garden were removed to be smelted down for guns etc. dug up the lawn to plant vegetables, dig for victory .was the slogan, tighten our belts the sacrifice was worth it for victory. Workers were encouraged with songs like.

> Praise the Lord and pass the ammunition
> Praise the Lord were on a mighty mission
> Praise the Lord and pass the ammunition
> And we'll all be Free.

The war for us was very much something we heard about over the radio we had very little experience of bombing raids in Edinburgh just the occasional stray bomb, one I remember demolished a block of flats in Leith. We were kept up two nights running while enemy planes flew overhead to bomb Clydebank in the west, but in the main the air raid shelter became a play area for us children. I kept rabbits in two hutches at the top of the vegetable patch, one I called Stoory and the other Patchy. On one occasion we caught a hedgehog in the garden and put it in the air raid shelter. That night the siren blew just as I was falling asleep, my mother shouted to get up and make for the shelter. I suddenly remembered and called back "You can't go in the shelter a hedgehog is in there".

My father was a member of the British Union of Fascists and never wavered in his admiration of the party leader Sir Oswald Mosley. He attended the Earls Court meeting in June 1939 the great rally for peace.

I remember him saying on his return just before Mosley began to speak you could have heard a pin drop in that vast arena of 20,000 people. That meeting and many others of course were never broadcast and only those in attendance knew what was said. I remember a programme on television a few years ago when five of Mosley's men were interviewed. One of them said that if he had been told that a few months on (in fact September of that year) the country would be at war he could not have believed it such was the enthusiasm shown at the meeting. The British people of course were never presented with the alternative to war, the vast majority had their ear to the wireless set and only one view was expressed there and that was war with Germany. The opposition voice was surpressed and during the conflict, those opposed to war with Germany in public life were thrown into jail. My father was arrested but did not go to prison. I don't know why, he never talked about it, and I can remember the day of his arrest well. It was almost on my twelfth birthday in May 1940, and playing in the street with other boys I saw this low slung Wolsley car draw up in front of the house two plain clothes men get out and went up to the front door. My mother let them in. They were there for a while, perhaps twenty minutes and then they left. I assume my father was arrested at the shop because he was not at home. My mother said afterwards that she had heard that fascists were being arrested under 18B regulations, so she searched the house and destroyed every piece of evidence she could find. A letter had arrived that morning which she hid on her person, the men apparently not taking the trouble to search her. Later that day, in the afternoon, I was some distance from the house when I saw my father in his car; overjoyed at seeing him I threw my arms in the air and shouted 'Daddy'. He pulled up the car stepped out and chastised me for not being with mummy and 'why was I playing in the street?" He returned to the car, banged the door and drove off. My high spirits were soon dashed and I felt a little bitter at his attitude. Looking back now, I can understand. I should have been at home at such a time of family crisis, but I think it would have been my mother's way to make little of it and allow the day to pass as normal as possible. During the war we listened to Lord Haw-Haw every night (William Joyce). He was entertaining with his distinguished voice and style and sometimes had a man, Amery, helping him. His take-off of life in Britain during the war was so accurate he must have had a good scriptwriter. Joyce was the only one of the British Fascists to be tried for treason and hanged, but he was, of course, of Irish-American descent, so his defence was that he could not be tried under British law. His broadcasting career came to an end as he faded away like the old soldier, the radio signal becomming weaker until he was heard no more. We had close friends in the 'Movement', you could almost say they were family ties and many happy times we spent together. When the men were let out of prison we attended one wedding in a Church of Scotland church on the west side of the city. The couple eventually having four children, but we have now lost contact, I often wonder where they are.

Well, the war wore on with bigger bombs more destruction until the end and the revelations of Jews murdered in gas chambers, the vast square miles of devastated German cities (More bombs dropped on one city, Berlin, than was dropped by enemy planes on Britain over the whole period of the war) showed the ugliness of war and when it is over the whole mess has to be cleaned up. The defeated countries, Germany and Japan, have done rather better post-war in strengthening their economies, but then they want to forget the war, put it behind them and look to the future, whereas we continually harp back to the days of conflict trying to relive these memories and to experience again 'Our Finest Hour'. But a country continually looking back has no future, war solves no problems merely creates more problems, more difficult to solve. War should be seen as a bad way to settle disputes between countries and when it is over, a new approach should be made to ensure a peaceful future. If we are attacked then that is different, we must defend ourselves, pacificism has no place in a Christian society, but we were never attacked or threatened attack by Germany. Churchill said when war was declared in September 1939. "This is not a question of fighting for Danzig or fighting for Poland. We are fighting to save the whole world from the pestilence of Nazi tyranny and in defence of all that is most sacred to man."

Thus it was a moral issue and this was shared by the other leaders of the political parties in Britain and that is the view that prevails to this day.

Britain and France made the declaration of war following the German land forces invasion of Poland on 1st. September 1939.

Eighteen days later the Russian army invaded Poland from the east so we were now in the position of having made a declaration of war on one country because of its act of aggression but not on another who had made a similar act of aggression and against the same country. I think therefore our action was too hasty and if we had delayed we would have seen the wisdom of our strategy by not fanning the flames of war. If one reads Hitlers speeches it is quite clear who Germany's enemies were, the Bolsheviks and the Jews, not Britain nor France nor America. "Britain and America had nothing to fear from a rearmed Germany". so said Hitler in one of his speeches. The Germans had always wanted more space (Lebensraum) they feel land locked with powerful countries on either side France and Russia had signed a treaty of co-operation and friendship Britain had command of the seas. In Hitler's Mein Kampf he made it clear that German expansion lay to the east we need not have been confused as to Germany's intentions when Poland was invaded. Russia knew exactly what was happening hence the Russian invasion of Poland. Churchill according to his biographer said that he had been against communism all his life and had a record to prove it. He then went on to say that Communism and Fascism could be likened to the North and South poles there may be more polar bears at one end or more penguins at the other but they are equally repressive places to be and one should seek the temperate zones at all costs. If Churchill had lived up to that I would raise my hat to him but that is not what happened. We got involved in a war between two evils and so put our support behind one of these two evils. But in fact the war had nothing to do with right and wrong it was simply that Fascism was a threat to the Governments of the west whereas Communism was not, therefore in their eyes, Fascism was the greater evil. Well meaning individuals who claim that Nazi Germany's invasion of France, Netherlands and Scandinavia was a threat to them are mistaken it was merely an attempt by Hitler to strengthen his position in the west so that he could get on with the real war in the east. Of course it can be argued that Hitler made a big mistake in doing this because Germany was now in a situation she feared most having to fight a war on two fronts. It would have been better if he had dealt with the situation in the west first but then his attempt to do that was thwarted by our governments refusal to consider peace proposals put forward by the German government preferring to say that we stood alone against the might of Nazi Germany before America came into the war in December of 1941. The alternative to war was to rearm ourselves as strong as the potential enemy so that if there was an attempt at our shores we were ready with guns and armament equal or greater to that arrayed against us. Some would say were we just to lay back and let Hitler walk all over Europe? Well there would be one part of Europe he would not walk over and that would be Britain and we could have entered into agreements with France, the Netherlands, and Scandinavia warning Germany that any attempt to interfere with the sovereignty of any of these countries would bring us all into the war. To negotiate with Hitler would be considered by some to be impossible and yet he had no desire for war with England an agreement would have been possible but that of course would not have stopped the war between Germany and Russia. We had no interests in the continent of Europe no territory to defend many Europeans thought we were interfering in matters that were none of our concern. We certainly had enough to contend with at home and if the Empire was important we could have developed trade links and improved commerce to the mutual benefit of all countries. However the policy was that of total war following by the demand of unconditional surrender from the enemy and so prolonging the war and allowing Russian forces to enter Eastern Europe where they remained for 45 years. The war to defend freedom and democracy had meant for millions of people to lose these basic rights for nearly half a century. The greatest movement of peoples ever took place as millions fled in the face of the Russian advance into Europe. The discussion has raged on ever since. Did we leave the opening of the second front in the west too late and so let the Russians into Europe but it is all water under the bridge now.

I think one of the saddest things about recent British history is the fact that we were not able to produce new men to guide the country through the immediate post war years. After the Labour Government's policy of nationalisation merely put us further into debt resulting in more heavy borrowing which led to them losing the election in 1951 the Conservatives were returned to power with the same men who had taken us through the war, Churchill and Eden at the helm again and the country faced with serious economic problems. Churchill admitted that the problems facing the country in 1951 were more serious than the problems in 1940 they simply had no answer. Where were the new men, men with straight backs with a new vision with a hope for a better future, men with energy and drive they were not there just two old men with health problems without answers to the country's problems. Germany on the other hand, had new men Adenauer and the economic wizard Ludwig Erhard with his Social Free Enterprise policy to steer his country to a peaceful and prosperous future. In five years we were talking about the German economic miracle but there was no miracle at home just dependency on any source that would lend us money. This was Britain as a result of past policies pursued by the government it was not very nice but it was the consequence of the war and our post war efforts. 'We had to accept the situation and in the old British tradition muddle through. It was a great disappointment that we failed to produce men of the calibre of Adenauer of Germany or de Gaulle of France who were able to map out a future for their countries and then enter into a treaty of friendship putting war behind them as a way of solving problems. We, on the other hand, remain divided between our new roll in Europe and past loyalties to the old empire now called the Commonwealth. Our superior attitude will not allow us to accept our new roll in Europe even when faced with the fact that the old Empire has gone.

My maiden aunt in Shetland was not only a supporter of Winston Churchill she might well have been in love with him. She would draw herself up to her full height with pride in her eyes say "Great Man' But when Lord Moran's book came out "The Struggle for Survival" (I don't think she had read it probably read reports in the papers) giving a side to Churchill's life that surprised if not shocked some people, she looked at me sheepishly one day and said "I did not know he was like that". All admiration gone and probably thinking to herself that some of the things her older brother had been saying about this man may have been true,

My father's position on the war, along with his like minded friends, was that win or lose we would be worse off as a nation, that we would lose our empire and that communism would be the real victor in the conflict. This seemed to find an echo many years later when Churchill was in America shortly after resuming office in 1951.

January 7, 1952 Washington. Mr Churchill attacked with some-heat the decision to give the command of the Atlantic to an American. "I realise" he said "That England is a broken and impoverished power which has cast away a great part of its Empire and of late years has misused its resources, but these fellows (the Americans) bungled the U-boat war, and had to come to us for help. Speaking to Lord Moran later that day Churchill said "For five years these officers have had no lead. They have got into the way of agreeing to anything. There a deadlock over the Atlantic Command. I may have to submit. I might have to say to the Americans: I am sorry you will not release me from the agreement with the Labour Government." Lord Moran continued "Once more he spoke of the feeling of inequality; it was a cankering his mind, he grieves that England in her fallen state can no longer address America as an equal, but must come, cap in hand, to do her bidding."

"The Struggle for Survival"

Influences

Our aim should be to leave this world a better place than we found it, so we were reminded by our minister often as we grew up. I wonder if he could have said it about his generation, or could I say it of mine. I think we have to define what we mean by 'world'. We do not have influence over the whole world but only our own world which includes our nation, Europe, for Britain the Commonwealth and perhaps some of our allies. There is no doubt that the second world war influenced our thinking and attitudes and shaped our national character which prevails to this day. I think it can be said of our nation at least there has been a decline in religion among our people and certainly in our national life. Winston Churchill in talking to his doctor in 1955 thought that there had been a great decay in belief in his lifetime, and continued " It is bad for a nation when it is without faith."

I was standing as a candidate for the S. N. P. in 1978 when driving in the car with the constituency chairman he pointed to two well dressed young men walking along the street and said, "See these two men they are Mormon missionaries" I of course knew this and told him I was a member of the church now for two years. He was somewhat taken aback and when we stopped the car he pointed to a church building across the way and said, "See that building over there if you and I could come back in 50 years time that building and others like it will be gone. He confessed himself an atheist or as he put it a free thinker He also said that he had read the Book of Mormon and could not see how the Mormons were christian as there was so little of Christ in the book. Leaving that aside for the moment irreligion has become a way of life for many people in the United Kingdom, how has this come about? And to suggest that this is true for the rest of the world is simply not so. A programme on television recently on Nothern Ireland showed how deeply religion has woven its way into the fabric of life there even more so than Southern Ireland. In Utah most people will be at Church on Sunday and religion plays a big part in the lives of most people living there. In America a television channel is devoted to spiritual matters where every denomination is given air time. Why is it that in the U. K. religion has become such a backwater and why are church organisations not fighting for air time or trying to promote their own television channel. Every home in the country has the TV box in the living room whether the occupants can feed themselves or not it is having tremendous influence on the lives of people and if the churches are not represented there then I believe they are failing in their missionary responsibilities. A religious channel was set up recently to broadcast to Europe with the promoters saying 'Why should Satan have it all his own way' Exactly, why indeed?

The struggle between good and evil is always present, it is a war that never comes to an end. Cecil B. de Mille, the Hollywood film director, said that life was a struggle between good and evil and all subjects and situations are examples of this struggle. The sadness following failure as well as the triumph following success are all examples of the battle sometimes we win sometimes we lose we are all involved none of us can escape. We are all prone to justifying our position and convincing ourselves that we are right but,truth will prevail right is right and wrong is wrong and we will pay the penalty for our wrong doing and receive the blessings for our righteous living there is no escaping this. However there is a way we can overcome evil, there is a way we can escape evil influences although it might be more accurate to say lessen evil influences.

To reject wise council is a sure way to fall and if this should happen to an individual there is only one way back. To stay on the straight and narrow path requires study and adherence to principle. A nation that has fallen has gone off the straight and narrow path and it is only by having a close look at the situation to determine where things have gone wrong that matters can be put right. Alas for our poor nation right seems to have triumphed because we won the war, but it is precisely because of that we are unable to progress in peace time. As long as you put faith in war as a way of solving problems you will solve no problems. It is only by rejecting war putting it behind us as a sad part of our history and looking towards higher goals and ways of achieving these goals will we then make progress. I sometimes squirm when I hear religious leaders and writers talk about Mr Winston Churchill being a great man. Is a man great when he takes his country from a position of strength to one of weakness and dependency on other countries. One writer on religion described him as being supported by all three keys to success, sound judgement, immense industry and excellent health. I wish men of the cloth would ask the question, 'was Churchill a Christian?' I print below some extracts from Lord Moran's book 'The Struggle for Survival' which throws some light on this.

Churchill and Religion

August 17, 1944
Lord Moran, (Churchill's doctor) Tonight when I was alone with Winston to my consternation he said. 'I want you to tell me your story about the monastery. No I'd like to hear it. I have always tried to understand the point of austerity' — *a broad grin appeared* — *'though I cannot claim that I have seriously practised it' When Lord Moran had finished his story about becoming a monk Winston seemed abstracted. At length he said. "I suppose you believe in another life when we die" 'When I did not answer he pressed me' "You have been trained in logic. Tell me why you believe in such things" Lord Moran concluded 'I had the feeling that he too wanted desperately to believe in something but from what he said he did not find it easy'*

July 2, 1953 Chartwell
'Winston spoke of death. He did not believe in another world; only in

'black velvet' — eternal sleep'

March 1,1955 House of Commons
'What ought we to do? Which way shall we turn to save our lives and the future of the world? It does not matter so much to old people ; they are going soon anyway , but I find it poignant to look at youth in all its activity and ardour and, most of all to watch little children playing their merry games , and wonder what would lie before them if God wearied of mankind.'

May 3, 1955 Chartwell
Churchill 'I believe the spirit of man is immortal. But I do not know whether one is conscious or unconscious after death' Moran 'I told him what Ike had said to me, that freedom itself meant nothing unless their was faith'. Winston thought there had been a great decay in belief in his lifetime. 'It is bad for a nation when it is without faith,' he muttered Moran. 'Isn't that true also of the individual?' Winston did not answer.

March 7,1958 France
Moran. 'As I was leaving Winston's room I picked up a Bible. 'Do you read it' I asked him. He did not answer for some time. Then he said: 'Yes I read it but only out of curiosity.'

After Churchill's stroke in 1953 Lord Moran said. "Though Winston has been determined to get well, if it lay in his power, death must have seemed very near to him as he lay helplessly watching the creeping paralysis advancing over his body. What passed through his head I could only guess. He had always made light of religious things, but could a man of his cast of mind, in his eightieth year, with death around the corner, find peace of mind in pagan beliefs".

Lord Samuel said of Churchill in 1954. "I don't think he has ever taken any interest in speculative thought, in philosophy or religion". Lloyd George had great insight into human behaviour and in his War Memoirs he gives his view of Churchill thus :

"I felt that his resourceful mind and his tireless energy would be invaluable under supervision. That he had vision and imagination, no one could doubt. That is why I thought he ought to be employed. I knew something of the feeling against him amongst his old Conservative friends and that I would run great risks in promoting Churchill to any position in the Ministry; but the insensate fury they displayed then later on the rumour of my intention reached their ears surpassed all my apprehensions, and for some days it swelled to the dimensions of a grave ministerial crisis which threatened the life of the government. I took the risk, and although I had occasionally some reason to regret my trust, I am convinced I was right to overrule the misgivings of my colleagues, for Churchill rendered conspicuous service in further increasing the output of munitions when an overwhelming supply was essential to victory. As to Churchill's future, it will depend on whether he can establish a reputation for prudence without losing audacity". I don't think it can be said in any way that Churchill was prudent. Some may argue that this criticism could be levelled at all the war leaders and I would have to agree. That the policy of total war where civilise christian people behaved more like barbarians resulting in the holocaust was unquestionably the result of rashness in policy decisions. The terrible crimes that took place in central Europe during the last year of the war were the collective responsibility of all the participants it is easy to put the blame on one side but in the end all were culpable.

The war was fought for freedom no doubt about that. When the question was asked why? Why are we fighting this war? The answer was always the same 'We are fighting for our freedom' and people would say well yes we must have our freedom that is worth fighting for. But as General Eisenhower said freedom itself means nothing unless there is faith and it is this word faith that is sadly missing in our national life today. A talk given by one of our General Authorities in April 1994 I print below:

THE PATH TO PEACE
President Thomas S. Monson

As we turn backward the clock of time, we recall that some fifty-five years, ago a desperately arranged peace, a conference of peace, convened in the Bavarian city of Munich. Leaders of the European powers assembled even as the world tottered on the brink of war. Their purpose, openly stated, was to pursue a course which they felt would avert war and maintain peace. Mistrust, intrigue, a quest for power doomed to failure that conference. The outcome was not 'peace in our time,' but rather war and destruction to a degree not previously experienced. Overlooked, or at least set aside, was the hauntingly touching appeal of one. who had fallen in an earlier war. He seemed to be writing in behalf of millions of comrades — friend and foe alike:

In Flanders fields the poppies blow
Between the crosses, row on row,
That mark our place; and in the sky
The larks, still bravely singing, fly
Scarce heard amid the guns below.

We are the Dead. Short days ago
We lived, felt dawn, saw sunset glow,
Loved and were loved, and now we lie
In Flanders fields.

Take up our quarrel with the foe:
To you from failing hands we throw
The torch; be yours to hold it high.
If ye break faith with us who die
We shall not sleep, though poppies grow
In Flanders fields.

Are we doomed to repeat the mistakes of the past? After such a brief interval of peace following World War I came the cataclysm of World War II. In fact, this June will mark the fiftieth anniversary of the famed landings of Allied forces on the beaches of Normandy. Tens of thousands of dignitaries and veterans will flock to the scene as the landings are re-enacted. One writer observed, 'Lower Normandy has more than its share of [hallowed dead. Their bodies] lie in graves from Falaise to Cherbourg: 13,796 Americans, 17,958 British, 8,658 Canadian, 650 Polish, and around 65,000 Germans — more than 106,000 dead in all, and that is just the military, all killed in the space of a summer holiday." Similar accounts could be written describing the terrible losses in other theaters of combat in that same conflict.

The famed statesman, William Gladstone, described the formula for peace when he declared: "We look forward to the time when the power of love will replace the love of power. Then will our world know the blessings of peace."

World peace, though a lofty goal, is but an 'outgrowth of the personal peace each individual seeks to attain. I speak not of the peace promoted by man, but peace as promised of God. I speak of peace in our homes, peace in our hearts, even peace in our lives. Peace after the way of man is perish able. Peace after the manner of God will prevail.

We are reminded that "anger doesn't solve anything. It builds nothing, but it can destroy every thing." The consequences of conflict are so devastating that we yearn for guidance over a way to insure our success as we seek the path to peace. What is the way to obtain such a universal blessing? Are there prerequisites? Let us remember that to obtain God's blessings, one must do God's bidding".

Yes indeed 'To obtain God's blessings, one must do God's bidding.' I am reminded of a poem I learned at school and have never forgotten, one of Milton's sonnets.

> Licence they mean when they cry freedom,
> For he who loves that, must first be wise and good,
> But from that mark how far they rove we see,
> For all this waste of wealth and loss of blood.

'How far they rove we see' from the way God would have us live our lives. As for Churchill's question as to what would happen to the little children if God wearied of mankind it is significant that he said this in one of his last speeches made in the House of Commons. The fact is that God will never weary of mankind, it is not God that has turned his back on mankind but mankind that has turned their backs on God. God will answer prayers only if we live by his laws that is the eternal laws we call the commandments. If we do not do this then it will seem to many as it does seem to many that there is no God. I think

Eisenhower's view that freedom itself means nothing unless there is faith is correct. Far too much stress has been put on this word freedom after all what is freedom, freedom to do right freedom to do wrong there has to be a moral dimension to the word freedom. The devil was often depicted as a little green man with horns on his head but latterly he has been seen as a little man in uniform with a black moustache and giving the arm salute. Evil takes many forms and I think many of our church leaders and political leaders were mistaken in thinking that in getting rid of the evil of national socialism that the world would then go forward to heights of moral strength and glory. It did not happen and our country and people have been in a confused state in all of these years following the second world war. Evil takes many forms and may I present a list as given in the book 'The Miracle of Forgiveness' written by one of our church leaders Spencer W. Kimball

Murder, adultery, theft, 'cursing, unholiness in masters, disobedience in servants, unfaithfulness, improvidence, hatred of God, disobedience to husbands, lack of natural affection, high-mindedness, flattery, lustfullness, infidelity, indiscretion, backbiting, whispering, lack of truth, striking, brawling, quarrelsomeness, unthankfulness, inhospitality, deceitfulness, irreverence, boasting, arrogance, pride, double-tongued talk, profanity, slander, corruptness, thievery, embezzlement, despoiling, covenant breaking, incontinence, filthiness, ignobleness, filthy communications, impurity, foolishness, slothfulness, impatience, lack of understanding, unmercifulness, idolatry, blasphemy, denial of the Holy Ghost, Sabbath breaking, envy, jealousy, malice, maligning, vengefulness, implacability, bitterness, clamour, spite, defiling, reviling, evil speaking, provoking, greediness for filthy lucre, disobedience to parents, anger, hate, covetousness, bearing false witness, inventing evil things, fleshliness, heresy, presumptuousness, abomination, insatiable appetite, instability, ignorance, self-will, speaking evil of dignitaries, becoming a stumbling block, and in our modern language, masturbation, petting, fornication, adultery, homosexuality, .and every sex perversion, every hidden and secret sin and all unholy and impure practices.

These are transgressions the Lord has condemned through his servants. Let no one rationalise his sins on the excuse that a particular sin of his is not mentioned nor forbidden in scripture.

Well there is enough to be going on with there. It is a sobering thought that if we put too much stress on one evil to the exclusion of all else then another evil will manifest itself in a different form we have to be constantly on our guard and to submit ourselves to wise council such as given above.

If faith is an important aspect of our national survival how do we obtain faith? People are quick to point out the divisions in the Christian church but I would like to suggest there is more that unites the churches than divides them. They all accept the Bible as the Word of God and the writings of the prophets and apostles contained therein, the ten commandments, Christ's sermon on the mount and the atoning sacrifice of the saviour that is his death and resurrection. Yes they differ on baptism, ordination of women to the priesthood and the modern day acceptance of homosexuality. Faith is the operative word common to all denominations therefore we must know what faith means. Paul says 'Faith is the substance of things hoped for and the evidence of things not seen' but that does not answer the question how do we obtain faith. Another of our church leaders Ezra Taft Benson has stated that 'Obedience is the first law of heaven'. therefore to obtain faith we need to be obedient to some law and that law for christians is the ten commandments. Freedom itself means non compliance with any law or principle except the law of the land and even that to be bent or broken if possible. As the poet Robert Burns stated in one of his poems;

> I'll no say men are villains a'
> The real, hardened wicked,
> Wha hae nae check but human law,
> Are to a few restricked:

But if we fight a war on the principle of freedom itself and nothing more then the wicked might not be 'to a few restricked' but may engulf a whole nation.

Politicians and potential leaders of nations make great sway of their quest for freedom but we ought not to lose site of the higher forms of freedom as mentioned in the Presbyterian hymn;

Make me a captive, Lord, and then I shall be free;
Force me to render up my sword, and I shall conqueror be,
I sink in life's alarms when by myself I stand;
Imprison me within thine arms, and strong shall be my hand.

We ought never to give up the fight for real freedom. Eisenhower soldier and politician,knew what real freedom was, Churchill politician and war leader knew it was bad for a nation when it is without faith, they were not men of the cloth but leaders of nations. Some would say these are old fashioned values they are in fact eternal principals that will never change with time. Our troubles as a nation whether economic or otherwise can all be traced to a moral decline, there is only one way back, can we rise to the challenge.

CHAPTER 12

The Conflict Ancient and Modern

The Book of Morman is said to be a second witness of Jesus Christ and also like the Bible it is a history book. The introduction says in part:-
"The book was written by many ancient prophets by the spirit of prophecy and revelation. Their words, written on gold plates, were quoted and abridged by a prophet-historian named Mormon. The record gives an account of two great civilations. One came from Jerusalem in 600 BC and afterwards seperated into two nations, known as the Nephites and the Lamanites. The other came much earlier when the Lord confounded the tongues at the Tower of Babel. This group is known as the Jaredites. After thousands of years, all were destroyed except the Lama~nites, and they are the principal ancestors of the American Indians."

I would like to look at one of these civilations the one that came from Jerusalem in 600 BC and afterwards split into two nations called the Nephites and the Lamanites.

The book is also known as a history of a fallen people. There were constant wars between the Nephite and Lamanite peoples. The Nephites were the good people who worked hard, "did till the land and raise all manner of grain and of fruit and flocks of herds and all manner of cattle of every kind". The Lamanites on the other hand lived for no other reason than to war on the Nephite peoples. In every conflict the Nephites won the contest fighting a defensive war against their attackers,but,in the last conflict after one thousand years of history the Nephites were wiped out and the Lamanites triumphed. Why did this happen?

The Nephites were a covenanted people who had promised to keep the Laws of God,but,they broke that promise when they attacked the Lamanites in the belief that this would bring the 1,000 years conflict to an end. But, in attacking the Lamanites they broke their promise and so received no help from the Lord; and so the good people did become extinct which fulfilled a prophesy given 400 years earlier.

It does not follow that good people will stay good, they do sometimes abandon their principles or come under the influence of unholy and masterly leadership. In fact the names Nephite and Lamanite eventually began to define the good from the bad as there were both peoples on either side. There was continual crossing from one side to the other.

The end of the war at Cumorah is described thus:

"And now it came to pass that after the great and tremendous battle at Cumorah, behold the Nephites who had escaped into the country southward were hunted by the Lamanites, until they were all destroy ed.—— And behold also, the Laminites are at war one with another; and the whole face of the land is one continual round of murder and bloodshed; and no one knoweth the end of the war."

Would that description be any different from the scenes that prevaled in central Europe near the conclusion of the second world war. When we witnessed the Jewish inmates of the prison camps the vast square miles of destroyed German cities scenes of carnage and destruction seldom seen before evidence of man's inhumanity to man. The vast movement of peoples as they fled in face of the Russian advance into Europe and then the Allies quarreling among themselves and the threat of a third world war hanging over our heads. and for what purpose — to destroy an evil.

It is therefore not surprising that Churchill discovered in the post war years that "England is a broken and impoverished power" and according to Lord Moran "He (Churchill) grieves that England in her fallen state can no longer address America as an equal etc. etc.

It may be arguable that the British were a covenanted people but we were a Christian nation that might be expected to apply Christian values in our national life, that our leaders would be men of Christian principle if not we are leaving ourselves open to the charge of hypocrisy. War is the exact antithesis of all that the Christian conscience stands for, "To love God and your neighbour as yourself". But if we pursue a policy of war first making a declaration of war then rejecting all peace proposals put forward by the other side engaging in total war and then demanding from the enemy unconditional surrender these are attitudes that are totally unchristian.

In every war previous to the last conflict the Nephites were fighting a defensive war and they won every battle but their attitude changed. 'They began to boast in their own strength etc." They therefore broke the commandments they had covenanted to keep and so received no help from the Lord. Their doom was sealed and they became a fallen people. Mans' interpretation of good and evil does not necessarily conform with that of deity. Winning a war does not mean that right has triumphed over wrong. Were the Lamanites right because they won the war against the Nephites? The Nephites became a fallen people because they abandoned their principles, Mormon refused to be their leader because of their wickedness and abominations. It is therefore evident that principle and the upholding of these principles is important and whatever argument seems justifed if it conflicts with the law entered into we must turn aside from it. To go to war against an evil because it is evil is wrong to defend ourselves against an evil is not only a right but a duty, pacifism has no place in the christian society.

Thinking young people in our community are aware of a feeling of despondency among our population, why should this be?

After the terrible carnage of the second world war many nations have adopted the attitude, never again. For many the climate of opinion is, let us now stop conflict, put it behind us and try cooperation instead. You would expect this to be a wide spread feeling after the devastation and destruction in a major war of lives and property; and this has happened in Europe with the advent of the Common Market and following that the formation of the European Parliament. Yet Britain has never entered into a spirit of hope for a better world. We were taken into the European union like a lamb to the slaughter. We are still spending not millions but billions on defence projects and people are asking the question, where is the enemy? Is it likely that another war on the scale of the last world war is imminent? Surely it is obvious the advent of atomic weapons has changed the situation and war on a large scale using such weapons is unthinkable.

After all, what did the cream of our manhood make the supreme sacrifice for, that the conflict should continue or cease? When we make the promise, 'to remember them' what are we remembering to do? Surely to make a better world for people to live in. The spirit of hope for a better world does not prevail among our people; the concept of faith hope and charity, has no part to play in our national life. Until we resurrect these concepts the feeling of despondency will continue, and we will always be below par as a nation. We will remain in bondage until we face the truth for it is the truth that shall make us free.

Excerpts from The Book Of Mormon and The Bible on war

ALMA CHAPTER 48 V 14 - 15

Now the Nephites were taught to defend themselves against their enemies, even to the shedding of blood if it were necessary; yea, and they were also taught never to give an offence, yea, and never to raise the sword except it were against an enemy, except it were to preserve their lives.

And this was their faith, that by so doing God would prosper them in the land, or in other words, if they were faithful in keeping the commandments of God that he would prosper them in the land; yea, warn them to flee, or to prepare for war, accord ing to their danger.

3RD. NEPHI CHAPTER 3 V 20 - 21

Now the people said unto Gidgiddoni: Pray unto the Lord, and let us go up upon the mountains and into the wilderness, that we may fall upon the robbers and destroy them in their own lands.

But Gidgiddoni saith unto them: The Lord forbid; for if we should go up against them the Lord would deliver us into their hands; therefore we will gather all our armies together, and we not go against them, but we will wait till they shall come against us; therefore as the Lord liveth, if we do this he will deliver them into our hands.

PROVERBS CHAPTER 14 V 16

A wise man feareth, and departeth from evil: but the fool rageth, and is confident.

ROMANS CHAPTER 12 V 19 - 21

Dearly beloved, avenge not yourselves, but rather give place unto wrath; for it is written, Vengeance is mine; I will repay, saith the Lord.

Therefore if thine enemy hunger, feed him; if he thirst, give him drink: for in so doing thou shalt heap coals of fire on his head.

Be not overcome of evil, but overcome evil with good.

CHAPTER 13

Righteousness Exhalteth a Nation
Proverbs 14:34

Controversy springs up from time to time over our National Anthem. It is not a good anthem and I will tell you why. It idolises one person who occupies the position on the Throne by shear accident of birth. I am not anti-royalist but a National Anthem should mentioned the ideals, aspirations, beliefs and principles of the people and as some others do the beauty of the land. The King or Queen after all, although head of the state and occupying the throne is a servant of the people and aspires to these principles in the same way as the man in the street. 'God save the Queen' is all the National Anthem says and that seems to make God subordinate to the Queen as He is being asked to run around to save the Queen. The Queen should also be able to sing the National Anthem and feel a sense of nationalism and loyalty in serving these ideals as ordinary citizens do, it is the people and their well being after all that is important. We are Christian people, a Christian nation, there is no harm in mentioning Christian values and trying to aspire to them. Our second National Song 'Land of Hope and Glory' contains these Christian values. 'Land of Hope and Glory' Chorus

Land of hope and glory, mother of the free,
How shall we extol thee, who are born of thee?
Wider still and wider shall thy bounds be set
God, who made thee mighty, make thee mightier yet
God, who made thee mighty, make thee mightier yet.

Dear land of hope, thy hope is crowned, God make thee mightier yet
On sovreign brows, be loved renowned once more thy crown is set
Thine equal laws by freedom gained, have ruled thee well and long
By freedom gained, by truth maintained, thine empire shall be strong.

These words express the ideals we stand for strive for are prepared to
defend and if need be fight for. Freedom is a cause we can all share,
Christian and non Christian alike, therefore 'Land of Hope and Glory'
should be our National Anthem as it has a wide appeal in its words to
the vast majority of our citizens. 'My Country 'tis of Thee'. The words
of this song can be sung to the tune 'God Save the Queen'. There is
more substance in the words although liberty and freedom are given
prominence it does say in one line, 'Let mortal tongues awake; Let all
that breathe partake; Let rocks their silence break', a call to all, to wake
up and speak up and out, to be fearless and brave, to speak our minds
and of course to defend freedom of speech.

We live in a divided society in Britain, the workers vis. the capitalist
entrenched in our two political parties of Labour and Conservative. You
could say that loyalty to the Queen or Throne is a unifying factor and
the Queen and Royal Family on their trips abroad represent all the people but I am advocating a national song we can all sing with feeling for
the great ideals this country stands for. It would give guidance to our
young people and too, for the more mature also in that at least we know
our goals and objectives and are reminded of them every time we sing
the song. I think it would have a steadying force and a sobering effect
on the young and would give meaning to our daily tasks and provide for
many our "reason d'etre". 'God save the Queen' has a hollow ring
about it and is merely a show of loyalty to the Queen. There is no harm
in singing it for that purpose, however we need a song that will instil
moral strength and character that will inspire the people with words to
reach higher goals. What are the things we strive for? Fairness, equality

for all? A Zion society where there are no rich and no poor? I have seen this in some degree in other lands. For example in Denmark I visited with Scout group (1958) the people would tell us with quiet pride 'in Denmark we have no slums, old houses yes, but no slums'. Well that is something to know that everyone in the country at least has good property and hopefully a good home. Shetland is a one class society where there is no rich and no poor. For many years there was no crime on the Islands, the people are liberal in outlook and are happy in there island home. It is true the discovery of oil has changed Shetland and there is division now with some earning big money in oil related projects. But these were examples of a society with a sense of fairness and equality in their structure. But we need to have goals of fairness and equality before we can strive for them and that is what is lacking in our national life. Our leaders talk of a caring society but the only tangible thing is the welfare state which we enjoy where plenty of hand outs are available if you know how to get them. Welfare is better expressed in providing work for our citizens so that they can earn their living. Our divided society has not brought us economic strength, since the 30s we have been struggling. Other countries have been more successful in the civilised world to share the wealth around. Unity of purpose therefore is essential and ideals of a better world need to be expressed and sung before we can attain them.

MY COUNTRY TIS OF THEE
1 My country 'tis of thee, Sweet land of liberty, Of thee I sing; Land
      where my fathers died,
Land of the pilgrims' 'pride, from every mountain side Let freedom
      ring'!
2 My native country, thee, Land of the noble free, Thy name I love; I
      love thy rocks and rills,
Thy woods and tempted hills. My heart with rapture thrills like that
      above.
3 Let music swell the breeze and ring from all the trees Sweet
      freedom's song.
Let mortal tongues awake; Let all that breathe partake;
Let rocks their silence break, The sound prolong.
4 Our fathers' God to thee, Author of liberty To thee we sing;

Long may our land be bright with freedoms holy light.
Protect us by thy might. Great God our King!

The twelfth Articles of Faith of the Church of Jesus Christ of Later Day Saints says "We believe in being subject to kings, presidents, rulers, and magistrates, in obeying, honouring and sustaining the law". The Scoutmaster's dilemma in not being able to live up to the Scout Promise (Chapter 2) is one we are all faced with as citizens of our country and members of the Christian community. Those who become conscientious objectors and refuse to go to war should they be considered men of courage and the rest of us weak and easily led astray?

America entered the second world war in December 1941 after the Japanese attacked the naval fleet in Pearl Harbour. The first conference of the Church after the declaration of war was held in Salt Lake City in April 1942 and the first presidency put out the following message:

"The whole world is in the midst of a war that seems the worst of all time. The Church is a world-wide church. Its devoted members are in both camps. They are the innocent war instrumentalities of their warring sovereignties. On each side they believe they are fighting for home, country, and freedom. On each side, our brethren pray to the same God, in the same name, for victory. Both sides cannot be wholly right; perhaps neither is without wrong. God will work out in His own good time and in His own sovereign way the justice and right of the conflict but he will not hold the innocent instrumentalities of the war, our brethren in arms, responsible for the conflict. This is a major crisis in the world-life of man. God is at the helm".

This I feel is the right stance any church should take in time of war. The churches cannot always stop war but to support a policy of war where killing takes place on a massive scale, not only service men but civilians also, is a questionable stance to take. Christians fighting Christians, what does God looking down from above make of it all.

If I may quote a passage of modern day scripture from our Doctrine and Covenants Section 130 verses 20 and 21.

"There is a law irrevocably decreed in heaven before the foundations of this world, upon which all blessings are predicated — and when we obtain any blessing from God, it is by obedience to that law upon which it is predicated".

This means that although we are free to make choices for ourselves we are not free of the consequences of the choices we make. Do good and we will receive blessings, do wrong and we will receive penalties. This applies to every man and woman who plants their feet on this earth. It applies to nations in the same way as individuals. Of course there are lots of grey areas in between. Some are more right than wrong some more wrong than right. As a nation how do we gauge our rightness or wrongness. An article written by one of our General Authorities of the Church headed 'The Lord will Prosper the Righteous' he says:- "The Lord has demonstrated throughout the generations that when the inhabitants of the earth remember Him and are obedient to His direction, he will bless them not only with spiritual blessings but with material abundance as well".

When I was in America in 1993 a young mother living in Utah a member of the church said, 'The American way of life is the most perfect on earth it is not perfect but the most perfect'. I did not answer her but she may have had a point, does prosperity go along with righteousness? Shortly before I went to the U.S. an article appeared in the American 'Time' magazine headed 'Boom Time in the Rockies' it began:- While most of the U.S. is suffering from the blues, or stuck in an outright funk like California, the six states along the spectacular spine of the Rockies — from Montana in the north through Idaho Wyoming, Colorado and Utah to New Mexico in the south are prospering happily. This is the good news belt. Since 1991, its economic growth has regularly exceeded 5%, in contrast to an anaemic 1% in the rest of the U.S. The article did say the area has had its time of boom and bust in the past, but it would be nice to think that in a region of people with strong religious convictions, the Lord does prosper the righteous.

The moral stance our country Great Britain took at the beginning of the second world war and pursued relentlessly until the war was over extracted great sacrifice from our people and country and left us only a shadow of our former selves. This was confirmed by Winston Churchill after he resumed premiership in the 1950s when in America talking to his doctor and colleague, Lord Moran, he said "When I have come to America before it has been as an equal. If, late in the war, they spoke of their sacrifices we would retort by saying that for a year and a half we fought alone; that we had suffered more losses". He sighed deeply.

"They have become so great and we are now so small. Poor England! We threw away so much in 1945".

Peace and prosperity is a well worn cliche but it still holds good, one never hears of war and prosperity. War is only a short time in the life of man, one day it comes to an end and life continues on. Whatever the outcome — God is at the Helm.

CHAPTER 14

In Search of Paradise

The missionaries knocked on the door of a man in his fifties. In conversation with the young men he did not want to listen to their message but was prepared to accept and read the Book of Morman. Calling back some time later the missionaries were surprised to hear him say yes he had read the book, yes he knew it was the word of God, and yes he would be baptised. Norman a single man was full of enthusiasm when he first joined becomming assistant ward clerk and a stake missionary a few weeks later. I got to know him quite well. He was an electrician and supervised the installation of electrical fittings on new buildings a job which took him all round the world. One of his first assignments took him to the Shetland Islands which he used to talk about quite a lot. However he spent most of his time in Africa and eventually to South Africa. After reaching the top of the tree and becoming secretary to the board of directors, living in a large house with servants, being driven around in a limousine, more money than he could handle he walked away from it all becoming a tramp in Johannesburg, losing all his possessions walking about all night to be safe from attack and sleeping during the day. His reason for this about-turn,he said,was that the higher you got the more wicked men became and he wanted no part of it. He was left to deal with competition and the instructions were, destroy this company, destroy that company. Norman was a good-looking man with bright blue eyes and he had ladies running after him all his life, but because of an unhappy childhood Norman had no intentions of getting married. I believe this was the reason he fell away from the Church because of the importance the Church attaches to family. One sunny Sunday morning in Jo'burg while living rough he watched people dressed up in their elegance making their way to church and was moved to write the following poem. He said if he had written it as a member of the L.D.S. Church he would have written it differently but I think it is a good poem and reproduce it below.

IN SEARCH OF PARADISE

Throughout this Earth, each Sabbath Day,
Dressed in their finest clothes
Millions of Pilgrims make their way,
To where? God only knows
Each one, brought up to believe
His is the one, true, faith
Their church is right, all others wrong,
They believe this, to the grave.
On looking back through history,
It's so hard to conceive
Man killing man, and torturing,
Because of their belief.
Each convinced in his own way,
That God was on their side
And even when losing, they would pray,
That He may turn the tide.
O Lord! I wish Thou would'st explain,
Is't Thine Eternal Plan?,
Men kill each other in Thy Name,
Until the end of man?,
'Tis clear to me, as clear can be,
That e'er since time began,
Religions, Churches, and Taboos,
Were all devised by man.
In man's insatiable lust for power and wealth,

Those are the means unto that end, he's used with stealth
For this I know, and this I know full well,
To keep man under — threaten him with Hell.
Poor devout souls, while here on Earth,
Each one in his own way,
Is buying shares in Paradise,
For when they pass away.
Fools! Heaven and Paradise, and Purgatory, and Hell,
Are in minds of men,
And with us here and now.
This I have found full well.
Why wait for Death,
While here in Life, is Paradise enough?,
Just look now at your fellow man,
And who can fail to see.
For some, life is a living Hell,
For others, Purgatory.
Gaze not upon those ones too long,
For infectious, it can be.
Instead, go seek the happy ones,
And then you'll realise,
That they have found this Heav'n on Earth,
Yes — even Paradise.
For Paradise is Here and Now,
And Happiness is free.
Go forth, and grasp it while you can,
Take this advice from me.
The Rose — once all the petals blown,
Forever dead shall be.
Be not involved in politics or strife,
But go and seek the simple things in life
Look close at nature, and you won't go wrong,
List' while the birds greet each new day with song,
And flowers, bathed in the early morning dew,
Resplendent in their coats of every hue,
With fragrance suggestive of romance,
Toss their heads, in gay, abandoned dance.

And even the tiny ants, in their own way,
Welcome each day, with renewed energy.
On this Fair Earth, why is it only man,
Should be the one, who would upset Thy Plan?
For those of you who would wish to be free,
To enjoy the simple things of life, with me.
Try not to change this Earth of ours, but see
If you can't just accept your Destiny.
And then one morn, on opening your eyes,
You will discover — you're in Paradise'

A SHETLAND HOLIDAY

It s Early Morning on the Mainland
So Quiet so Peaceful and Still
On a July Morning in the Dawning
Another Day another Thrill

The Sun shines on Land and Sea
The Town still sleeps no one About
On a July morning before the Yawning
Peace shall Reign let no one Doubt

The Sun shines on the distant Hills
The Sea reflects the shimmering Rays
On a July morning in the Dawning
Arise and Wake ye Banks and Bays

A Ships siren breaks the Silence
The overnight Ferry moves to Berth
On a July morning early Dawning
From her Ocean travels to Mother Earth

Another morning though calm and serene
Low Cloud covers the Hills
On a July morning giving Warning
A different Day the Weather Wills

The Sun shines on the Island of Mousa
The afternoon brings a brighter Day
The Broch, Sea Lions and Ship wrecks
We wish we had longer to Stay

The weather forecast is "Dull and Wet"
There's a Trip to Tronda, Burra and Tingwall
And Scalloway Castles on the Way
Just the thing to beat the Rainfall

To visit friends not seen for Long
To meet and chat is our Desire
To view the Sound and see the Voe
Recalling memories we never Tire

The sea all around sees calm and Fair
A Journey for us is in Store
The Island of Noss we are at a Loss
To describe what we saw or say More

A Stroll to Lerwick in the Sunshine
To the Library, Museum and Town Hall
To climb the Clock Tower and Discover
How to be Big and walk Tall

A Visit to the North Isles by Coach
On a clear day and Warmed by the Sun
To visit friends and Relations
A Good Day in more ways than One

It's Goodby to Hjaltland the Holiday is Over
The Old Rock is also its Name
A bit sad to be leaving Shetland
Only the Memories now Remain.

A LAMENT ON THE SUMMER OF 1985

The weather is bad, 'tis very sad
The season it seems has gone quite mad
How are we to see it through
Can't say yea, must say boo.

The weather is bad it's gone quite mad
Or maybe it's just taken a fad?
Will we ever see the sun again
And so see less of this awful rain?

The weather is bad, the worst we've had
Caught in the storm I feel a cad
The rain keeps runnin' doon ma' breeks
I haven't felt them dry for weeks

The weather is bad, 'Stay in your pad,'
The best advice I ever had
He who ventures unprepared
Returns wishing he'd never dared.

The weather is bad the forecast is mad
Low pressure it seems is keeping it bad
The weather men say, 'Sun out today,'
We smarten up and feel quite gay.

The weather is bad whatever they say
It's been like this since the month of May
Rain rain will you go away
And never come back another day.

The weather is bad, I am going mad
It seems so sad, but I am going mad
I can only look forward to the winter time
And feed the meter with my well earned dime.

The weather is bad 'tis very sad
To get an opinion I asked old dad
He looked at me with experianced eyes
There is a reason try to be wise.

The weather is bad there's been a depression
Maybe in this we are taught a lesson
Do not expect too much from life
But be prepared for trouble and strife.

The weather we know reflects our moods
But we never seem to get out of the woods
Won't summer come and cheer our souls
Before the winter starts and the football goals.

The weather is bad the gloom persists
And we ask the question, 'What did we do for this?'
We look each day, for the skies to clear
Really it's been an awful year.

The weather the weather, it's always the weather
The opening remarks when greeting each other
May come the day before this year is out
We can say 'tis summer without a doubt.

CHRISTMAS,
NINETEEN HUNDRED AND EIGHTY FIVE

Christmas is comming it's that time of year
When folks gather and friends draw near
To celebrate a birthday in their own way
Of a baby born and in a manger lay .

Christmas sounds are pleasant to hear
Carols and jingle bells gladden the ear
Brass bands and organ and trumpet sounds too,
Children singing in the way children do .

It's Christmas time, where are the Reindeer?
Santa needs them his sledge to steer,
Children are waiting their gifts to receive
Wondering what Father Christmas will leave .

Christmas is comming have no fear
The story is old and very clear
How a saviour came into the world
The flag of faith and hope to unfurl .

It's Christmas time lets get into gear
Round the shops and in the windows peer
Thinking of our friends at Christmas time
Hoping they are well and feeling fine .

At Christmas time we shed a tear
For those that are gone and we loved so dear
The joy for the moment is tinged with sadness
As we remember their presence and loving kindness .

Just as the water over the weir
Flows day by day year by year ,
The spirit of Christmas fills our souls
Our heart jumps up like the spring time foals .

Not like old Scrooge with his frown and jeer
Cursing his existance while on his rear
Bah/ to people the short and the tall
Bah/ to Christmas he says to all.

Christmas comes like Edward Lear
A book of nonsence every year,
So some would like us to believe
No faith no works for man to weave.

It's Christmas time now is'nt it queer,
People are happy and full of good cheer
Parties and fellowship make a fine sound
Why can't it happen all the year round .

So Christmas has come you will have to veer
To miss the spirit and the abundant cheer,
So come along and sing the song
Let the music play and sound the ding dong.

The last verse on Christmas come and hear
All simple folks and nobleman peer
The family has gathered to hear the rhyme
Love came down at Christmas time.

FAITH

'What is Faith', the Enquirer Asks
As in his ignorance he Daily Basks
What is it that Without Works
All Around us Lurks

Is it something we can Grasp
Or something Hidden Behind a Mask
Is it something we can See?
Just how does it affect Me?

Has it something to do with Hope
Or how to get hold of a Bar of Soap
Is it something to do with Knowledge
Or how to pass Your Exams at College

It seems as Mysterious as the Foreign Legion
This name that follows True Religion
I wish I could find some Relief
Is it something to do with Belief?

"Faith is the Substance of things Hoped For"
So says Paul our Brother and Neighbour
And "The evidence of Things not seen"
Now what exactly does that Mean

The Saviour Himself Showed the Way
As Those infirm in their Chamber Lay
And others in need came to Him
To make them Well in Life and Limb

The Leper came unto The Saviour
His need was great he did not Waver
"Can'st though make me clean" he asked
Jesus touched him and his Illness Passed

The Synagogue where Jesus Taught
Where People meet and sick friends Brought
A man held out his Withered Hand
To have it Healed He'd make a Stand

"Is it lawful to do Good on the Sabbath"
The Pharisees Asked in their Contained Rath
Then Jesus Looked upon his Brother
Restored the Hand Whole as the Other

Though many Troubles face Mankind
Some weighed down with Troubled Minds
Yet these cares and woes need not Be
If only we had the Eyes to See

In God we find Hidden Strength
Why be content with just One Tenth
Through his Laws and Commandments
    He has Prepared the Way
Where Saints may find the everlasting Day

NETHER TOON

When sauntering through the Isle of Yell
And beauty spots you have in mind
Just keep your findings open wide
Untill you come to Nether Toon

When comming back from Wester Firth
Where scenery wild with waves that boom
If tide be out you wade across
And linger on at Nether Toon

When sailing down the Voe of Gloup
The awesome hills on either beam
But beauty here is far surpassed
When you arrive at Nether Toon

When frost and snow obscure the earth
And songs of birds desert the scene
But yet the cruelest cut of all
To blot out lovely Nether Toon

When summer comes with fragrance round
And life is bright with flowery bloom
The fairest spot upon the earth
You will behold at Nether Toon

The winy whopes jets overhead
The blackbirds hops. and sings their tune
The Ladian hovers in the breeze
All sing the praise of Nether Toon

In simmer dim when couples walk
With future hopes and lights at green
In ardent tones they seal their truss
For ever more at Nether Toon

And when through life should tension rise
And clouds to intervene
They'll ne'er forget the pledges swopped
That far off night at Nether Toon

In sixtreen days when boats went out
Some twenty miles from Blue Mull sound
By sail or oar they made the land
And found their haven at Nether Toon

At Johnamas time they stayed ashore
With harmony and glee around
That nights of gladness they enjoyed
With songs and mirth at Nether Toon

The lasses came from far and near
For to make do they just made room
Get on your jumps its Johnsmas night
To dance and sing at Nether Toon

Before the time of beauty queens
For cosmetics there was'na room
The ladies made their own deterge
They burnt the kelp at Nether Toon

In bygone days when lights were dim
And coly lamps just pierced the gloom
When oily saundy produced the fuel
That lit the lamps at Nether Toon

When touring in the town of Gloup
To whalrie and heather bloom
To see the Kirks and anciens Ha'
And then the gem of Nether Toon

When self indulgence seem supreme
The faction rage with threats of doom
When at a premium self and gain
We think of placid Nether Toon

Empires they may rise and fall
And cities great not what they seem
But hamlets they will aye be dear
Such one is lovely Nether Toon

A POEM TO COMMEMORATE THE GLOUP
FISHING DISASTER OF 1881

In those lone isles there is a spot
Where happy memories go,
A pretty spot mid barren hills,
Its name is called Gloup Voe.

Though quiet now, this place was once
Where happy people dwelt
With honest labour's rich reward—
Contentment, which is wealth.

The fishing fleet was stationed here,
Their goods were bought and sold,
A happy sight, the faces bright
Of people young and old.

But like the dreams of one brief night
This happy scene was gone,
It passed away one July day
In eighteen eighty-one.

This day the boats all turned once more
To take the seaward route;
With music in their rowing oars
The fishing fleet set out.

With thoughts of wives and children dear
Each hardy fisher goes
With quiet, reverend trust in God
Such as the fisher knows.

With powerful strokes the boats speed out
Amid the scenes of yore,
Familiar shores sink down from view,
That shall return no more.

The fishing ground with care is found
By landmarks called the medes,
Their lines are set with tacfful skill
Which ripe experience breeds.

'Twas then the fatal gale came on
A storm dark and wild.
The boats are tossed by the raging sea
Like toys by an angry child.

As steel is forged by furnace fire
So danger brave men make,
These rugged men to perils bred
Are not afraid or shake.

To cut their lines and run for land
Before the awful gale,
Their slender mast raised on high,
To hold a close-reefed sail.

With skilful hand his boat to steer
A lion's heart within,
Each dauntless skipper seats himself
Beside the helm pin.

The mind cannot depict the scene
Nor shall the pen relate
What fateful billow proved the end
Of this last race with fate.

At morning dawn relations stand,
With anxious, tearful eye
Look out upon the surging waves
That meet the lowering sky.

Survivors come, hopes rise and fall
All doubts are quickly o'er,

Six boats containing each six men
Are now to come no more.

Survivors said God's work they knew
His power to give and take,
Their pathway through the mighty waves
Was like an open gate.

The perished sleep in nameless graves
Where many heroes lie;
These humble toilers of the deep
Were not afraid to die.

They bravely went at duty's call
On life's rough stormy sea,
Though tossing billows mark their graves,
Peace, peace their rest shall be.